MW01100208

Sowing Beside All Waters

Emma Leslie Church History Series

PLACIDIA CARRIED OFF BY THE RIOTERS

Page 40

EMMA LESLIE CHURCH HISTORY SERIES

Sowing Beside All Waters

A Tale of the World in the Church

BY

EMMA LESLIE

Illustrated by
W. J. MORGIN & E.W.

"Blessed are ye that sow beside all waters..."
Isaiah 32:20

Salem Ridge Press
Emmaus, Pennsylvania

Originally Published
1875
Nelson & Phillips

Republished 2007
Salem Ridge Press LLC
4263 Salem Drive
Emmaus, Pennsylvania 18049

www.salemridgepress.com

Hardcover ISBN: 978-1-934671-06-1
Softcover   ISBN: 978-1-934671-07-8

PUBLISHER'S NOTE

Throughout the long history of the Church, faithful men and women have had to fight not only against attacks from outside the Church but also against error from within. In *Sowing Beside All Waters* we see some of the challenges that faced the Church in the fourth century. We can also see that in their zeal to fight against certain errors they laid the groundwork for others and that in their eagerness to spread Christianity they allowed dangerous compromises with the world.

In our eagerness to fight against errors within the Church we must be careful that we do not make the same mistakes. We must always have the Bible as our final standard as we stand strong against all attacks.

There is also the testimony of the effect that mothers can have on the world. Through the prayers, love and godly examples of Monica and Arethusa, the mothers of Augustine and John Chrysostom, Christianity and the world have been blessed and changed forever.

In the end we see that it can be just as challenging to remain faithful to God in times of blessing as it is in times of persecution. My prayer is that no matter what our situation, each of us will remain faithful to the Lord Jesus Christ.

Daniel Mills

November, 2007

HISTORICAL NOTES

A number of important historical figures from the third and fourth centuries A.D. are mentioned in *Sowing Beside All Waters*. Here is a brief summary of these people:

Diocletian: Diocletian began his reign as Emperor of Rome in A.D. 284. During his reign he established many important reforms that helped to stabilize the Roman Empire, but for the last two years of his reign he instituted what has since become known as the Diocletian Persecution. During this brutal persecution thousands of Christians were martyred and countless more were tortured for refusing to renounce their faith. In A.D. 305, Diocletian, in poor health, voluntarily stepped down as Emperor, the only Roman Emperor ever to do so.

Constantine: Following the reign of Diocletian, there was a great deal of fighting and scheming to determine who would rule the Empire, with Constantine at last emerging victorious in A.D. 324. Constantine credited his victories to a vision telling him to place the first two Greek letters in the name of Christ on his soldiers' shields, rendering them impervious to defeat. Constantine soon moved the capital of the Roman Empire from the city of Rome to the city of Constantinople and made Christianity the official religion of the Empire. He also called the **First Council of Nicæa**, in A.D. 325, which was the first worldwide meeting of bishops since the time of the Apostles in the first century. This council was called to resolve the dispute over the doctrine taught by a man named Arius. Contantine died in A.D. 337 and was succeeded by his three sons.

Arius: Arius was a Christian priest in Alexandria who taught that, rather than being eternal, Jesus Christ the Son was created by God the Father. Although his teaching was condemned by the First Council of Nicæa, Arianism continued to spread and caused divisions in the Church for hundreds of years. Arius died in A.D. 336.

Athanasius: As Bishop of Alexandria, Athanasius worked throughout his life to refute the teachings of Arius. Because of this, Athanasius was exiled several times but each time was allowed to return to Alexandria. Athanasius died in A.D. 373 at the age of eighty.

Eusebius: Eusebius was Bishop of Cæsarea and one of the first Church historians. He was a friend of Emperor Constantine and an important participant in the First Council of Nicæa. Eusebius died in A.D. 340.

HISTORICAL NOTES

Saint Anthony the Great: Anthony was an Alexandrian monk who in A.D. 284, at the age of thirty-four, decided to sell his possessions and become a hermit. Over the remaining seventy years of his life, Anthony lived almost exclusively in the deserts of Egypt. A history of his life was written by Athanasius and his example caused many to choose to leave the world and form monastic communities.

Julian: Born in A.D. 331, Julian was a nephew of Emperor Constantine. Julian's life was threatened, and many of his relatives were murdered, by Constantine's sons as they each claimed the throne following Constantine's death. As a result, Julian rebelled against Christianity and when the army declared him Emperor in A.D. 361 he attempted to reinstitute the worship of the Roman gods. Julian was a successful military leader but died in A.D. 363 during a campaign against the Persian Empire.

John Chrysostom: John, the future Bishop of Constantinople, was born in A.D. 347. He studied under the pagan philosopher, Libanius, in Antioch but was baptized into the Church in A.D. 370. John then spent the next eleven years of his life in seclusion as a monk. Finally, in A.D. 381, he returned to Antioch and began his public speaking and teaching. In A.D. 398 John was appointed the Bishop of Constantinople. There he denounced the luxury of the clergy and the sinful lifestyles of the Christians, winning him many friends but also many enemies. One of these enemies was Eudoxia, the wife of Emperor Arcadius. In A.D. 403, Eudoxia erected a statue of herself for public adoration which John promptly denounced. She quickly banded together with rival bishops and convinced Arcadius to have him banished. John died in the mountains of northern Turkey four years later. He was given the title "Chrysostom" which comes from the Greek word meaning "Golden-mouthed".

Augustine: Augustine was born in northern Africa in A.D. 354 to a devout Christian woman. Despite this, he left the Church and embraced a Persian religion called Manichaeim. During this time he also lived a very immoral lifestyle. Highly educated, Augustine taught at various schools throughout the Roman Empire. Then, in A.D. 386, he read Athanasius' account of Saint Anthony and decided to leave Manichaeism for Christianity. He was baptized, returned to Africa, sold his possessions, gave the money to the poor and founded a monastery. In A.D. 396, he became Bishop of the city of Hippo, a position he held until his death in A.D. 430. His writings and teachings have had a profound impact on the Church, including inspiring reformers such as Martin Luther and John Calvin.

IMPORTANT DATES

A.D.

313 Constantine's edict ending the Persecutions published; the Cross chosen as the Standard of Rome

315 Punishment of the Cross abolished

324 Constantine becomes sole Emperor

325 First Council of Nicæa

327 Athanasius elected Bishop of Alexandria

328 The seat of Empire transferred from Rome to Byzantium, renamed Constantinople

331 Heathen temples demolished

337 Death of Constantine

347 John Chrysostom, Bishop of Constantinople, born

354 Augustine, Bishop of Hippo, born

363 Julian attempts to rebuild the Temple of Jerusalem

Nicæan Creed of A.D. 325

"We believe in one God the Father Almighty, Maker of all things visible and invisible; and in one Lord Jesus Christ, the Son of God, begotten of the Father, Only-begotten, that is of the substance of the Father; God of God; Light of Light; Life of Life; very God of very God; begotten, not made; of the same substance with the Father; by whom all things were made, both things in heaven and things in earth; who for us men and our salvation descended and became flesh, and was made man, suffered, and rose again the third day. He ascended into heaven; he cometh to judge the quick and dead. And in the Holy Ghost. But those that say there was a time when he was not; or that he was not before he was begotten; or that he was made from that which hath no being; or who affirm the Son of God to be of any other substance or essence, or created, or variable, or mutable, such persons doth the Catholic and Apostolic Church anathematize."

The Eastern Roman Empire

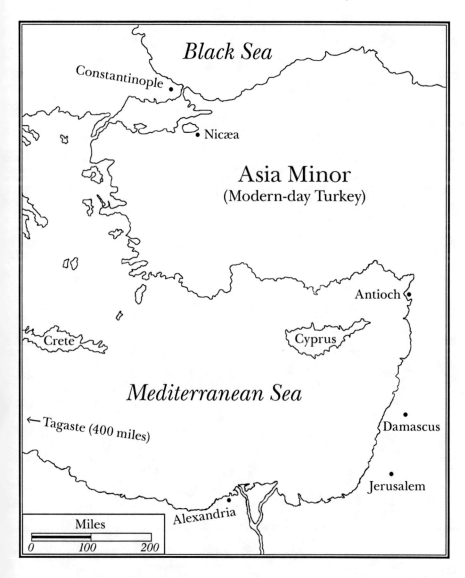

Black Sea

Constantinople •

• Nicæa

Asia Minor
(Modern-day Turkey)

Antioch •

Crete

Cyprus

Mediterranean Sea

← Tagaste (400 miles)

Damascus •

Jerusalem •

Alexandria •

Miles

0   100   200

CONTENTS

ILLUSTRATIONS

Sowing Beside All Waters

Sowing Beside All Waters

Chapter 1

Alexandria

THE morning light was brightening the waves of the blue Mediterranean as they rolled into the spacious harbor of Alexandria, bearing on their crests a small flotilla of imperial galleys. They had been seen approaching, and now that the harbor was gained a loud cheer rang from the busy quays. The countless masts were each decorated with a flag, while high above all others—higher than the proud Roman eagles—was hoisted the emperor's new ensign of the cross; for times had greatly changed, and the struggling infant Church of Christ, no longer persecuted, was now patronized by the reigning emperor, Constantine.

The imperial messenger just arrived in the

FLOTILLA: *fleet of small ships*
GALLEYS: *ships propelled by oars*
QUAYS: *docks*
ENSIGN: *flag or emblem*

harbor was the court preacher, Hosius, Bishop of Cordova, and he bore letters from Constantine himself to Alexander, the aged primate or pope— he was the first to assume this title—of Alexandria, for this proud city vied with Rome itself in splendor and importance. There lay her riches in countless heaps, exposed to the rainless air— wheat waiting for shipment to Rome and Byzantium, and bales of merchandise crowding every quay, while in every nook and corner where customers were likely to be found sat a man behind a pile of fruit fresh from the fruit-boats close at hand. "Fresh watermelons! fresh figs!" cried one; while his neighbor sat lazily chewing the papyrus cane, and watching the approach of the splendid galleys.

"Times are changed since our late emperor, Diocletian, resigned the purple!" exclaimed an old man who likewise stood watching the gaily decorated vessels as they drew near.

"Yes, times are changed, thank God! for we can worship Him in peace without being carried before the prefect to have an eye put out or be maimed for life as the penalty."

"Yes, ye Christian dogs have it all your own way now. I've a great mind to turn Christian myself, for it is the only way to get on in the world," said the old man, with a half-drawn sigh for the good old times now so lately passed away.

RESIGNED THE PURPLE: *stepped down as emperor*
PREFECT: *a high Roman official*
LABARUM: *the banner of Constantine, decorated with Christian symbols*

The next minute there was another shout of welcome from the various quays, and someone exclaimed, "The emperor hath sent some of his new guards with the bishop!"

"New guards, indeed! as if these guards of the labarum could be more honorable than the old pretorians," said another contemptuously.

The news that some of the famous fifty, whose duty it was to guard the sacred ensign of the cross, had been sent on this errand to their patriarch seemed to please many, as adding not only to his but their importance. Their self-congratulations, however, in this respect were soon ended, for their deacon, Athanasius, who had come to represent the aged bishop and receive Hosius with all due honor and courtesy, quietly assured some that only one member of this famous guard had come, and he was on a visit to friends and relatives here in the city.

In spite, however, of this assurance the young man found himself the center of observation when he stepped ashore, for on cuirass and helmet shone this ensign of the cross in purest gold, and the Alexandrians had not yet become so accustomed to this former sign of shame and ignominy as to look upon it altogether unmoved. Never before, perhaps, had a guard of the labarum been seen in the metropolis of Egypt, and so the crowd might be excused for following the long line of ecclesiastics

PRETORIANS: *bodyguards of the Roman emperor*
CUIRASS: *leather breastplate*
IGNOMINY: *great public disgrace*
ECCLESIASTICS: *ministers or priests*

through the streets to the house of their patriarch, Alexander.

It was several years since the young guard had visited his native city, and as he looked round on the familiar scene—at the splendid esplanade and the Gate of the Moon by which they entered the city—at the Cæsareum and the world-renowned obelisks before it, one of which is still known as Cleopatra's Needle, and thought of the changes a few years had wrought not only in Alexandria but in all the world, his heart swelled with joy and thankfulness, for surely the Redeemer's kingdom must prosper, and all would soon bow to His scepter and own His name.

But these reflections were put aside by the bustle and crowd of palanquins, curricles, and laden asses all pushing their way up this, the main street, and frequently stopping the long procession of monks and presbyters who had come out to meet and conduct the emperor's messenger to their bishop.

When the ceremony of reception was over, and the young guard at liberty to leave and seek his own family, he was joined by his old friend, Athanasius. They had been brought up together under Alexander, but their paths in life had widely diverged since they sat together learning the use of the stylus; but the cause of the Master was still dear to the heart of each, although

ESPLANADE: *a large, level area for walking along the shore*
OBELISKS: *tall stone pillars or towers with pointed tops*
PALANQUINS: *covered litters carried on poles*
CURRICLES: *chariots pulled by two horses*

they could not see eye to eye.

"Thou art a soldier of the cross, but—"

"Nay, but thou too art a soldier of the cross if I mistake not, Athanasius; only thy weapon is not a sword of steel," interrupted his friend.

"True, Quadratus, but I would fain live in such peace as our holy hermit, Anthony. Only such men as Arius force us to use the Word of God as a weapon as well as a support and shield;" and the young deacon sighed as he thought of the peace of the desert, where he had spent days and nights in prayer and meditation with Anthony, without the interruption of a human face except that of a fellow-hermit.

"There hath been a sharp contest with this same Arius. I have heard somewhat of it, but would fain hear the whole matter from thee. Is it simply a question of learned disquisition, or is it one of great importance, Athanasius?"

"Great importance?" repeated the deacon, "Thou hast heard very little not to know that the peace, the well-being of the whole Church Catholic is imperiled by this Arianism; for do we not believe above all else that there is one God? and was it not for this denial of there being gods many and lords many that our fathers suffered and died?"

"And Arius, thy deacon, would teach that there is more than one God?" asked Quadratus.

PRESBYTERS: *elders*
FAIN: *gladly*
DISQUISITION: *a formal discussion or analysis*
CATHOLIC: *universal*

"Nay, Arius doth not teach this directly, but his doctrine must lead to this; and, moreover, it denies the divinity of our Lord Christ," said Athanasius. "But let me not hinder thee with the details of this now, for thou art anxiously expected at home. I saw thy mother yesterday, and she could talk of nothing but her soldier-son."

"Wilt thou not walk home with me? Thou wilt be welcome, Athanasius, as thou knowest."

But the deacon shook his head. "There is much sickness in Alexandria just now, and I must see that none lack either the bread that perisheth, or that which is able to save the soul alive. But I will see thee again shortly, and thou shalt tell me the news of the world beyond the great sea. Hasten homeward now, for I can see thou art longing for thy mother's embrace;" and with a pleasant smile Athanasius turned toward the poorer quarter of the town, while Quadratus took his way past the now half-deserted temple of Neptune toward his home, where his widowed mother was awaiting him.

"My son! my Quadratus!" were the next words addressed to him; and when his mother had kissed his bronzed cheek she pressed her lips reverently upon the golden cross that gleamed on his breast and whispered, "I am blessed above women, for one son is a soldier of the cross and the other a holy monk, and yet—and yet—"

"What is it, my mother; what wouldst thou say?" asked the soldier, seeing the tears in his mother's eyes.

"Nay, nay, my son; it is but my rebellious woman's heart longing for a sight of my Orestes once more," said the lady, trying to force back the tears, and looking up fondly in his face.

He pressed her to his heart more tenderly, and for a moment felt angry with his brother for leaving her. "He should have considered thy widowed state, and that he was the eldest, thy firstborn."

But to blame Orestes was to touch the widow's heart more keenly than anything. "Nay, nay, my son," she said, "he is right in his choice, and it would mar the sacrifice if he allowed any human love to draw him aside from his work of prayer and meditation."

"But, my mother, if all were to forsake their work in the world and fly to the desert, what would become—"

"Orestes did not forsake his work in the world," hastily interrupted the lady. "Thou dost forget that in the time of our late emperor there was no room in the world for Christians, and such as would preserve life and keep their faith were compelled to fly to the desert. Ah! blame not my Orestes that he refuseth to look on the face of his mother, for I was weak in those days, and it may be I should forsake my Lord again by trying to hold him back from his service in the desert."

"Well, I am glad the service I have undertaken calls me to cities rather than deserts, for it seemeth a nobler service to carry the conquering cross among men than—than—" and there

Quadratus paused, for he did not like to say anything disparaging of his eldest brother.

To his mother, however, that hasty pause was eloquent with praise of Orestes. "I know what thou
wouldst say, my son—that while thou art bearing
the conquering cross our Orestes is fighting the
battle for thee on his knees. I, too, will think of this,
Quadratus, when tempted to repine at his absence,
and the thought will comfort me for both of ye."

Seeing that the thought brought a smile to that
weary, careworn face, Quadratus would not contradict what had been said, as he at first felt in-
clined to do, but looked round the hall in search
of his sisters.

"Where are Placidia and Melissa?" he asked.

"Placidia leaves not her chamber, but will see
thee before thou dost leave Alexandria," said his
mother, a faint color stealing into her cheeks as
she spoke.

"My sister is ill—Athanasius told me there was
much sickness in Alexandria."

But the lady shook her head. "Nay, our Placidia
is quite well; but she, too, would fain leave the city
to dwell in the desert, and so—"

"She has become a nun," interrupted Quadratus. It was evident he had very little sympathy with
the choice of either brother or sister, and he asked
in a half-angry tone, "Hath Melissa forsaken thee,
too?"

"Thou dost forget Melissa hath gone to be the
light of another home," replied his mother, "or

DISPARAGING: *expressing a low opinion*
REPINE: *fret*

did our letters never reach thee?"

For a letter to miscarry was nothing very un-usual in those days, and so Quadratus had heard nothing of his sister's marriage, or of his mother's fear that her husband was little more than half a Christian; but he heard it now, and in listening to these particulars he forgot his vexation concern-ing Placidia and Orestes, until the slaves sum-moned them to the repast that had been ordered to be prepared in readiness for the coming of Quadratus, but which had been forgotten in the joy of meeting.

To see his mother sitting there with none but slaves to attend upon and care for her in her old age again raised the anger of the young soldier as he reflected upon the lonely life she must lead when he was away; and before the meal was over, he asked if he could not see Placidia at once.

"Thou art still my impatient Quadratus!" said his mother, smiling faintly, as the slaves brought a basket of fresh fruit and placed it in the middle of the table.

"My mother, doth not that basket remind thee of the old days when I used to lift Placidia in my arms, that she might see all the fruit from a dis-tance, and choose which fig she would have?" hast-ily interrupted Quadratus.

The lady smiled faintly. "Shall I ever forget those old days!" she said with a sigh. "Shall I ever forget the night when my husband was taken from me, to be brought back days after a sightless cripple! O,

REPAST: *meal*

Quadratus, I was weak in those days, but it was the thought of you, my children, who needed all my care, that made me shrink from a like punishment more than the pain itself."

"And the Lord Christ knoweth how strong the temptation was, and He who forgave Peter his denial will forgive thine, my mother," said the young soldier tenderly.

"I can never forgive myself, and when I hear our patriarch preaching on the Lord's great power and majesty, I feel half-afraid lest my sin is beyond His forgiveness."

"Nay, nay, but the power and majesty is all on the sinner's side; for great as these are, His love and compassion are greater. Fear not, my mother, thou hast confessed thy sin to Him, and He hath taken away the iniquity of thy sin. But tell me now, cannot I see Placidia at once? As thou sayest, I am impatient to see my sister once more, even though she be a nun."

"I will ask her to see thee, but I greatly fear she will refuse," said the lady, rising from her seat to go at once upon her errand.

"Nay, but tell her I will not be refused," said Quadratus. "Tell her I come as a messenger from the emperor, and his will is law in the Church as in the State now." This was said as a playful jest; but there was a truth underlying it which Quadratus had already begun dimly to see, and he wondered whether his friend Athanasius had seen it too.

Whether she took this message to Placidia or not he never heard; but a few minutes afterward a slave entered, saying he might ascend to the tower-chamber, and the next minute he was in his sister's presence.

But the calm, grave girl in the somber dress, not unlike a philosopher's robe, was very different from the gay, laughing Placidia he had pictured in his dreams, and as he looked at the still, pale, unmoved face he slowly uttered, "Is it my sister?"

"I am Placidia," she replied; but she did not draw a step nearer, and though a faint color stole into her face, she made no attempt to greet him, nor to show any emotion at his coming.

After a long and painful silence the soldier said, "I come to thee, Placidia, on behalf of our mother. If I could leave the service of the emperor I would come home at once to cheer her declining days, but thou, my sister, hast no other duty, and—"

"Hush!" interrupted the young nun; "I, too, have a service I cannot forsake—a duty higher than all others. For my mother's sake I have promised to abide here instead of retiring to the desert, but—"

"And thou dost think a life in a palm-leaf hut more noble and pure than helping men and women in the world—more pleasing to God than serving thy mother, who needeth the care of her children now in her days of weakness?" Quadratus spoke angrily, almost fiercely, but Placidia was quite unmoved.

"I have prepared myself for such temptations," she said calmly, and her mother seeing Quadratus was about to retort with another angry speech hurried him from the room.

Chapter II

Leaven

DISAPPOINTED as Quadratus had been in his interview with Placidia, he thought it would be best to defer his visit to Melissa for a few hours at least; but his mother was anxious he should go at once, and so, to please her, he set off to the fashionable quarter of the city where Melissa lived.

Quadratus had scarcely expected to see such a display of wealth and luxury as met his gaze in Melissa's household, but what struck him most painfully was, the contrast its courts presented to their own simple, unadorned home. Melissa expected him, and he was conducted at once to the inner court, the open part of which was adorned with a sparkling fountain, which, with the wind-sail stretched across the roof above, rendered it delightfully cool.

But it was not the fountain, nor the elegant columns of white marble and green porphyry that supported the colonnade, nor the orange and mimosa trees, with their chattering paroquets and

PORPHYRY: *a volcanic rock containing large crystals*
MIMOSA TREES: *flowering trees with fern-like leaves*
PAROQUETS: *parakeets*

sunbirds, that called up that grave look to his face as he entered, and then started as though he would retreat again at once.

His sister saw the start as she came forward to greet him, and she looked confused and embarrassed as she said, "Welcome, my Quadratus!"

But the soldier could hardly return the greeting for the embarrassment he felt, and forgetting for a moment everything else, he said, "This is not thy home—this is no Christian household, Melissa."

"Nay, nay, be not so hasty, my brother," said the young matron. "I am a Christian, as thou knowest, and my husband hath given up the public worship of the gods, and goes with me to church, although he is not yet baptized, and—"

"Our emperor is not baptized, yet he hath had all the statues of the demon-gods removed from his palace, that men shall no longer be tempted to worship them. But what do I see here? There is Juno, and Diana, and Jupiter, and Apollo, as though they still claimed and received the worship of the household." Quadratus spoke sternly—to Melissa it seemed unkind.

"We do not worship these statues," she said; "but my husband hath been used to see them, and his father, who lives with us, would be grieved to lose them from their places. The painting on the walls, thou seest, hath all been changed, and the legends of the gods have been replaced by Christian emblems, and from this picture of the shepherd carrying the sheep I can tell my little Alypus of the good Shepherd who giveth His life for the sheep." Melissa pointed to one portion of the wall as she spoke, and was going on to describe the rest, and the lessons she taught her little one from its frescoes, when Quadratus hastily interrupted her with the question:

"But what will thy little one think of the statues, Melissa? Art thou not afraid of the old idolatrous worship for thy boy?"

"He shall never learn them at all by their old demon names," said Melissa quickly. "My husband hath promised that I shall have my own way in this matter, and so I have called Jupiter Paul, and Apollo Peter, and while he looks at them I tell him of the works and labors of the apostles. Do not shake thy head and look so grave, for I often talk to Theon, his grandfather, by this means, and he will listen to Alypus as he sings the "Alleluia," although he will not go to church or converse with Athanasius when he comes."

"And thou art quite happy, my sister, surrounded by all these symbols of the old idolatry?" asked Quadratus.

"Nay, but they are not symbols of the old demon-gods to me," said Melissa; "they are beautiful works of art, and often remind me, as they do my child, of the apostles after whom they are named."

"But, Melissa, if—if they should come to be worshiped by and by in the place of God Himself—"

FRESCOES: *pictures painted onto wet plaster*

The suggestion, however, seemed so farfetched and so absurd to his sister that instead of looking serious she burst into a merry laugh. "Now, I know, thou hast been talking to Placidia, and it is she who hath put this notion into thy head," she said gaily.

"Is it Placidia's notion, too?" asked Quadratus.

"It would be, doubtless, since she would fain leave all that is beautiful and loving and home-like, to go and live in the desert. I have not asked her what she thinks, for it is rarely I see her now," said Melissa, throwing herself on a pile of cushions, and beckoning to her brother to follow her example.

Quadratus slowly seated himself near the edge of the fountain. "Athanasius hath not become a monk, as many feared," he remarked carelessly.

"No, this fuss about Arius, and his new, strange doctrine, hath drawn him into the busy life of the city, and he says it shall be his life's work to refute this heresy."

"Heresy!" repeated Quadratus; "that is a strong word, Melissa."

"Stronger words and harsher words than that have been used here in Alexandria during the contest; but he hath been cut off from the Church now by the assent of a hundred bishops, and so I hope the very name of Arius will soon be forgotten."

"But the emperor wants to make peace between him and our pope, Alexander. He thinks he hath

HERESY: *views that go against accepted beliefs*

been harshly judged; and Eusebius, Bishop of Nicomedia, hath exhorted all the bishops of the eastern and western cities to receive Arius."

"Then Eusebius must believe his doctrine—that Christ is not equal to the Father," said Melissa quickly.

"It may be so, for both were disciples of Lucian, the martyr, and I have heard that he held some such views, although he did not carry them so far as Arius."

"But will others, thinkest thou, espouse this heresy?" asked Melissa.

"They have done so. In Palestine, where Arius hath been journeying and preaching, he hath gained hundreds of converts, many embracing his views because of his master, Lucian, having held them."

"Then, Quadratus, if the Church of Christ is thus divided it cannot longer be called the *one* universal, Catholic Church. O, my brother, I did so love that name—the Catholic Church—the one Church—the universal body of Christians in all lands believing the same truths, worshiping the same God and Saviour, Jesus Christ. O, it is sad, it is pitiful; the persecution hardly over before they begin quarreling and dividing, and all but persecuting each other;" and the gentle, peace-loving Melissa could not refrain from shedding a few tears.

"Thou art not alone in thy regrets, my sister,"

ESPOUSE: *accept, embrace*

said Quadratus. "Our emperor is most anxious to restore peace, and it is for this Hosius hath come hither now, for nothing but the restoration of Arius can effect it."

"And he must renounce his doctrine—his false, unscriptural doctrine—or else not only our patriarch, but the city of Alexandria, will cast him out," said Melissa.

"I am not skilled in the learning of the schools, Melissa, and I know little of the science of hairsplitting, in which many so greatly excel; but I know that anger and bitterness are worse —are harder to convince, and do more positive harm than even a cruel persecutor like Diocletian."

"Quadratus, thou dost dare to call our holy patriarch, Alexander, more cruel than Diocletian!" exclaimed Melissa, with flashing eyes.

"Nay, nay, I said not so; but that if this division—this quarrel about Arius—was carried on in a bitter, angry spirit, it would do the Church of Christ more harm than a persecution from her foes," hastily explained Quadratus.

While he was still speaking, Lucullus, Melissa's husband, came in, leading his father by the hand, and the soldier was at once presented to them. The latest news from Rome was eagerly asked for by the old man, and Lucullus inquired whether there was any prospect of the present peaceful state of the empire continuing for any length of time.

HAIRSPLITTING: *excessive attention to differences*

Quadratus shrugged his shoulders. "There have been some whispers concerning the restlessness of Lycinius, and it is almost certain Constantine will make Byzantium the future capital of the empire."

"That will make little difference to us here at Alexandria, for both cities are dependent upon us for their corn supply; but what will Rome say to the change?"

"Rome hath already offended our emperor by the jests and lampoons made at his expense, because the gladiatorial shows are forbidden."

"Ah, it was a pity to put down the games," said Lucullus; "the people must be amused or they will amuse themselves, and who knows but it may be by driving the emperor himself from his throne?"

But Quadratus shook his head. "There is little fear of that," he said. "These games were wicked and debasing, and not only fostered a cruel temper in all men, and drew many away from useful and peaceful employments, but made brute force to appear more courageous than moral heroism. No man, either Christian or Greek philosopher, but is ready to admit this."

"I do not deny it," said Lucullus; "but I say it is dangerous to put down these savage games all at once. Christianity is only struggling into existence as yet, and hath many a battle before her, not only with the world and its old idolatries, but with the Jews, who are ever ready to seize an opportunity

LAMPOONS: *mocking statements*
DEBASING: *degrading*

of striking a blow at this new power; and the savage temper of our mob is the more easily roused if there is not the natural outlet for their ferocity allowed, as in the games of the arena."

"Then thou wouldst have Christianity pander to this ferocity instead of trying to subdue it," said Quadratus.

"No one could charge Christianity with introducing these games. Our people have been trained to this fierce love of bloodshed through centuries of such exhibitions as are all at once forbidden," said Lucullus, "and I would have the emperor proceed more cautiously."

"He is too cautious to please some; but in this matter most are agreed that, if this fierce love thou speakest of is ever to be rooted out, it can only be by the suppression of that which has fostered it—the games of the arena."

"And, meanwhile, we must suffer from the outbreaks of popular fury whenever it hath a decent excuse for venting itself in riots and tumults," said Lucullus, discontentedly.

"It is the penalty we must pay, I suppose, for these same centuries of lawless indulgence—another form of the Divine law—the sins of the fathers visited on the children," said Quadratus.

It was evident that Lucullus looked upon Christianity in a very cool, philosophical fashion, not at all in the way his wife and her family did. It had suddenly become the fashion, because the

PANDER: *aid in wrongdoing*
TUMULTS: *disturbances*

emperor had openly declared himself a Christian; and the high road to wealth and fame now was through the favor and patronage of a bishop, who but a few years before was poor and despised, and so Lucullus, like hundreds of others, had declared himself on the popular side, went every day to the Church of Alexandria, and married a Christian wife, as became a fashionable gentleman, and one of the merchant princes of the first commercial city in the world.

Quadratus could understand what his mother meant when she called him only half a Christian, but he had met with many such lately—many not so true, honest, and upright as Lucullus; and he left his sister's home feeling more assured of her happiness than when he entered, although he still entertained grave doubts of her wisdom in retaining the old idols in her household.

Before returning home again he turned toward the bishop's house, which was in the neighborhood of the stately Serapeum, with its four hundred majestic columns, one alone of which remains to tell us what the fellows of "Pompey's Pillar" might have been. The building was already grass-grown and half-deserted, for the worship of Serapis had declined so much the last few years that the priests and augurs began to fear its total extinction, and hated the Christians accordingly. Their hatred, however, was futile now, except in a time of public excitement, and then they

SERAPEUM: *a temple dedicated to the Egyptian god, Serapis*
AUGURS: *prophets*

readily joined with the Jews against the common enemy, as they chose to regard their fellow-citizens who had joined the Christians. One of the white-robed priests now stood near the entrance, and he scowled as he noticed the gleaming cross which shone so conspicuously on the breast of the soldier. "They glory in their shame," he muttered; "but their glorying shall soon end if Serapis hath any power in Alexandria."

Quadratus found that his peculiar dress as a guard of the labarum aroused more curiosity than was quite pleasant, and he resolved to lay it aside during the rest of his stay in Alexandria, except when he was called upon to attend the court bishop, Hosius, officially. Not that the sign of the cross was in itself uncommon now, for almost every Christian wore it as a sacred badge, and it occupied the chief place of honor in all the churches, and was regarded with a veneration only second to actual worship since it had been the accredited means of their emperor's conversion.

Before the archbishop's house was reached Athanasius overtook him with a small party of parabolani, or lay brothers, returning from their work of visiting the sick and poor, ascertaining their wants of body and soul, and ministering to their temporal and spiritual needs, for this care of the poor had been specially given to the Church, and a heavy burden it was sometimes.

Just now the young deacon, faint and wan from

VENERATION: *great respect or reverence*
ASCERTAINING: *seeing for themselves*
TEMPORAL: *physical*

want of food and the fever-tainted air he had been breathing, ventured to say something of this as he joined Quadratus. "I have sore misgivings too, sometimes, whether the patronage of the emperor is such a great gain to the Church of Christ," he added in a low whisper.

Quadratus looked surprised, almost shocked. "Not a great gain to the Church!" he repeated; "why, see the hundreds of worshipers who crowd the churches or basilicas, or wherever God is worshiped. Think of this, and compare it with the time when Diocletian ruled the empire—when Christians went in fear of their lives, when the churches were closed, and God's Word could only be taught in secret, and hundreds were slaughtered for refusing to worship the popular gods."

"Have I not thought of it, think you? Yet, still I sometimes question whether the sudden honor, and riches, and fame, have been wholly a blessing to the Church, and whether our emperor's patronage may not also crush our liberty and freedom—make the Church a mere appanage of the State at last."

"The danger is at least a remote one, and the actual gain is present and tangible," said Quadratus.

"But we have to guard against remote dangers," said Athanasius, "and that is why we have so vehemently opposed this doctrine of Arius."

"Our emperor will not wish the Church to receive a false doctrine," replied the soldier quickly.

BASILICAS: *large courtrooms or meeting places*
APPANAGE: *source of revenue*

Athanasius shook his head in a doubting manner. "Constantine is politic, and would have peace above all things," he said evasively.

"And is not Christ's kingdom one of peace and love?" asked Quadratus.

"The kingdom of heaven is first pure and then peaceable, and we have especially to guard against errors of doctrine in these days," said the young deacon, who was determined to struggle against this rising Arianism even if it involved him in a quarrel with Constantine himself.

POLITIC: *shrewd*

Chapter III

Brother and Sister

QUADRATUS was sitting with his mother a few days after the incident last noticed, in their own plainly furnished inner court, when the old lady suddenly broke a rather lengthy silence by saying, "I should like little Alypus to be baptized this Pentecost."

Quadratus started from his reverie. "He is two years old; I thought he had been baptized," he said.

"Nay, Melissa thinks it were better to be deferred lest he should stain his white baptismal robes with the sins of youth; but I—I long to see the child admitted a member of Christ's Church; and it may be I shall not live to see another Pentecost," said the old lady.

Quadratus looked into her face anxiously. "My mother, thou art not ill?" he exclaimed.

"No, not ill, my son; but I am an old woman, and my life, as thou knowest, hath been a troubled one, and—and—" but she paused and would not say more.

PENTECOST: *a holiday celebrated fifty days after Easter*
REVERIE: *meditation*

"My mother, what is it?" asked Quadratus in some alarm, kneeling at her feet and looking anxiously into her face.

She smiled as she smoothed the thick clustering curls of his dark hair. "Nay, nay, it is nothing—nothing but what must come sooner or later, and I have thought the last few weeks that it would be soon now—that my mansion was almost ready," she whispered.

Quadratus turned his head and gazed at the splashing fountain for a minute or two in silence. "This was why thou wert anxious to see Orestes once more," he said thoughtfully.

"I would fain have seen him once more here, but I shall not have to wait long, Quadratus, for there are no monks in heaven, and my Orestes will not shun his mother there. I am selfish, I fear, for I would fain keep thee with me, too, my son—keep thee and see my little Alypus baptized."

"I will stay with thee as long as possible," said Quadratus quickly; "and it may be Melissa will have the child baptized, unless—" and then he paused.

"What wouldst thou say?" asked the old lady anxiously.

"Her husband, Lucullus, might object."

"Nay, Lucullus is indifferent, and troubles not himself about such matters. He goes to church because it is fashionable and good for his trade as a merchant, but for all else I fear he believes little more in Christ than he does in Jupiter."

"But he goes to church, thou sayest, and often converses with Athanasius, so that he may learn to know more fully the truth of our holy religion," said the soldier.

"I trust it may be so, for he is in all else a true and just man, although he does laugh at the dispute with Arius, and often sings the songs from his Thalia."

"What is the Thalia?" asked Quadratus.

"A book of songs composed by Arius, after the pattern of those sung in honor of the demon-gods by the lowest and vilest here in our streets. Arius himself sings them and dances to them," added the old lady.

"And these songs are sung in our streets! Then I myself heard something of this as I passed through the marketplace this morning, and it was the same tune as that used for a revel dance. I heard these words quite plainly:

> 'God was not always Father,
> Once he was not Father,
> Afterward he became Father.'"

"That is how Arius hath been teaching all the city his evil doctrine—saying there was a time when Christ was not, and it is these discussions that cause many like Lucullus to stumble," rejoined the lady quickly.

"But even in the first age of the Church—in the time of the apostles themselves, men differed. One said I am of Paul, another of Apollos, and

REVEL: *festival*

another of Cephas, and it may be when Arius is dead others will arise to disturb the peace of the Church, so that it behooves everyone to look, not to teachers or bishops, however learned, but to Christ Himself. If we look more entirely to Him, trust ourselves to the teaching and guidance of His Holy Spirit more than to the opinions of men, it will be better for each of us, I am sure. I have learned this since I have been in Alexandria," added Quadratus.

His mother shook her head mournfully. "These are degenerate days," she said; "the golden age of the Church hath not dawned yet, I fear, as many suppose, although we have a Christian emperor on the throne of the Caesars."

To Quadratus this seemed like a reproach to his master, and as he was devotedly attached to him he turned the subject by saying, "Could Alypus be baptized before Pentecost, my mother?"

"Yes, the fifty days appointed for baptisms have not expired. If he were an adult he must of course be received as a catechumen first, and receive instruction for some time, but being an infant, and the child of Christian parents, there will be little difficulty in the matter."

"Then I will ask Melissa to present him for baptism at once;" and that there might be no further delay in the matter he rose as he spoke and prepared to go out.

Melissa, however, was not as easily persuaded in

DEGENERATE: *morally low*
CATECHUMEN: *student learning the basics of Christianity*

this matter as her brother expected. "I think it is cruel to baptize a child so young," she said.

"Cruel!" repeated Quadratus.

"Yes; if it is left until they are grown up the grace received is not so easily dissipated—they do not stain themselves with sin, and have to perform penances to cleanse it away again. That is why so many defer their baptism until they are grown up—until they are dying—that they may have all their sins washed away in the water of regeneration, and appear before God in their baptismal robes, clean and unspotted by the world."

Quadratus stared. "Then it is the water of baptism, and not the blood of Christ, that taketh away our sins," he said slowly.

Melissa colored. "It is the blood of Christ as well," she said; "but—but—"

"But that is not enough. Would you say that?" asked Quadratus sternly.

"No, no; thou knowest I do not mean that, Quadratus, but at our baptism we receive the pardon of our sins, and if we commit sins afterward we must do penance for them or they cannot be forgiven. Now how much better it is to defer our baptism until later, for sins committed after that are so much worse, and then the penance to be performed for every slip and mistake is often very tiresome."

"Sins are 'slips' and 'mistakes' now it seemeth, and repentance is 'tiresome'. Melissa, thou didst

DISSIPATED: *used up*
PENANCES: *voluntary punishments for sins committed*
REGENERATION: *being born again*

not learn that of our father and mother," added Quadratus.

The lady colored more deeply, and murmured something about "old-fashioned notions," but in a minute or two she said, "Everybody thinketh as I do about baptism."

"Everybody!" repeated her brother. "Nay, nay; our mother is most anxious to see thy Alypus baptized. Hath she told thee, Melissa, why she is so desirous of this?"

"Placidia hath been teasing her about it, I suppose," said Melissa, pouting.

"Nay, but she thinketh her days on earth are numbered, and she would fain see the little one admitted a member of Christ's Church here before she herself joins our Father above. That is why she was so anxious to see Orestes," he added.

"And Orestes ought to have come and seen her," said Melissa quickly. "But, Quadratus, is my mother ill?" she asked in a tone of anxiety. "I know she hath had several fainting fits of late, but she said there was little danger in them."

"She hath not told me about the fits, and she hath not complained of illness at all; but she thinketh her end is near. Wilt thou, therefore, deny her request—the last, perhaps, she may ever prefer?" asked her brother, solemnly.

"Nay, nay, do not say that; I cannot spare her yet," said Melissa, bursting into tears. "Alypus shall be baptized if she wisheth it. I will give

PREFER: *present*

notice that I wish to present him before Pentecost," she added.

"God bless thee! and Alypus too, Melissa. I am thankful, for my mother's sake, that thou hast decided the matter thus. And let me remind thee, my sister, that not the water of baptism but 'the blood of Jesus Christ cleanseth us from all sin.'"[1]

The news that little Alypus was to be baptized gave his grandmother heartfelt joy, and very earnest were the prayers offered on his behalf that he might receive a rich blessing from above, and not only be admitted a member of the Church, but continue a true and faithful servant in it until his life's end.

Baptisms could only take place in the cathedral church, and this was in the seaside suburb of Baucalis—the very church to which Arius had been appointed. This was the oldest church in Alexandria, and contained the tomb of Mark, and to this, during the fifty days preceding Pentecost, crowds might be seen wending their way. Just before the close of this sacred season, Lucullus and Melissa, with little Alypus, joined the throng in their curricle; while Quadratus and his mother came by another and more quiet road—she in her old-fashioned litter, carried by slaves, and he walking beside her.

They joined Lucullus at the church, and the old lady kissed Alypus fondly, who in his spotless white robe—emblem of the white raiment worn by

---

[1] I JOHN 1:7
WENDING: *making*
RAIMENT: *clothing*

the saints above, and the sinless state of those who are pardoned through the blood of Christ—looked as though he understood something of what was about to take place. "They brought young children to Jesus," murmured the old lady.

"Am I going to Jesus now?" asked Alypus, turning to gaze at the pictures on the wall as they entered the church.

There was a long line of penitents near the entrance—men and women who had by transgression soiled their baptismal robes, and now stood with downcast heads, mutely asking admittance to the church once more. They would stand here once, twice, thrice; on each time there was an assembly for some months, according to the enormity of their offense and as the bishop might direct.

Lucullus glanced at them as he passed. "I should pay someone to stand there for me if I could," he whispered in a half-jocular tone to Melissa.

The lady glanced at the silent row of mourners and shuddered. Suppose Alypus should have to stand there one day. But she put the thought from her the next moment; surely he would escape this somehow—perhaps someone else might do it for him, as Lucullus had suggested.

They had taken their seats near the baptistry, and little Alypus, in his long white robe, stood with the rest of the candidates on the other side of the font. A presbyter had lighted the candles at the stand where the roll of the Gospel was lying—not

PENITENTS: *people sorrowing over their sins*
HALF-JOCULAR: *half-joking*
FONT: *a bowl holding the water for baptism*

that their light was needful, for it was early morning; but various ceremonies had been added to the simple service of reading and prayer, and this was one of them. The candles were lighted to signify the light and joy revealed in the Gospel. A door at the side of the church was now opened, and the deacons and presbyters marched in, followed by the collectors and singers, and boys about twelve years old, each of them in white, and chanting the "Alleluia" as they passed to their places.

But before they had finished singing there was a faint sob heard, and on looking round Quadratus saw his mother sink down, pale and speechless, beside him. He would have carried her out at once, but Melissa said it was not necessary. "It is only a fainting fit," she said. "The excitement is a little too much for her;" and, chafing her hands as she spoke, she soon had the satisfaction of seeing her revive.

"Thou must not stay to the communion," she whispered; "when Alypus hath been baptized thou hadst better let Quadratus take thee home."

But the old lady shook her head. "I am quite well again now," she said, "and I will partake of this holy feast once with the child."

The service was very short, and then the bishop advanced to the font and the candidates drew near. One by one they were baptized; then the bishop laid his hand upon their heads, and breathing upon them, said, "Receive ye the Holy Ghost."

COLLECTORS: *those who are assigned to pray*
CHAFING: *rubbing*

A little later in the day the newly-baptized and other members of the Church gathered round the table of the Lord to commemorate the dying love of Christ for them, and to this sacred feast Alypus was led by his pious grandmother.

"We may never meet here again, my child," said the old lady, her voice quivering with emotion. "It may be I shall soon eat this in the kingdom above; but never forget this, Alypus, thy grandmother brought thee here, and thy grandfather was a martyr for the truth this feast proclaims. Melissa, thou wilt not forget to remind him of this. Thou wilt keep this day fresh in his memory, wilt thou not?" added the old lady, turning to her daughter.

Alypus, of course, could only look from one to the other, not understanding much of what was said beyond this, that the Lord Jesus loved little children, and had now taken him to be his own little boy, and that the piece of bread he ate and the wine he drank had been sent by the Lord Himself to assure him of this fact, and that he himself might never forget it.

"I belong to the Lord Jesus as uncle belongs to the emperor," lisped Alypus as he was going home, and repeating the words after Quadratus, for Melissa had taken charge of her mother in the litter, while Quadratus took her place in the curricle beside Lucullus.

"Mind thou art as faithful in thy service, too, as thy uncle, or else—dost thou know where they will

PIOUS: *devoted to God*

put thee if thou art naughty, Alypus?" asked his father.

The child shook his head. "Will they whip me?" he asked.

"Worse than that," said his father; "they will make thee stand in the vestibule of the church, as thou sawest those poor men today. I say," he added, turning to Quadratus, "I saw one of the richest men in Alexandria standing among the penitents today."

"Rich men commit sins as well as poor men, I suppose," said Quadratus drily.

"Yes, I suppose they do, but to see such a man as that before the church door!" and Lucullus shrugged his shoulders suggestively.

"He needeth repentance as much as the poorest, and it cost as much to redeem him," said Quadratus.

"Yes, I suppose it did; but if this penance could be done by proxy—by paying somebody else to stand there for thee—"

Quadratus looked greatly shocked, and yet what horrified him has since become a standing custom in that Church which calls itself Catholic and Apostolic, for it was by the adoption of the plan Lucullus recommended that the papal system of indulgences was introduced. Men who could pay to have the penance imposed for their sins performed for them preferred to do so, and this being a source of wealth to the Church became a prolific

VESTIBULE: *entrance hall*
PROLIFIC: *highly productive*

root of evil, and one of the greatest scandals of that corrupt organization.

This, however, was not foreseen then, but the suggestion of his brother-in-law made Quadratus very thoughtful during the rest of his journey homeward, and, to escape further discussion about this and the never-failing topic of Arius and his heresy, he left Lucullus as soon as he could, saying he wanted to go to church in the evening.

Chapter IV

The Riot

QUADRATUS went to the evening service in the church, where the patriarch preached to a crowded audience, many of whom evinced their attention and admiration of what was said by loudly clapping their hands. This was quite usual, so that Quadratus took little notice of the fact, but he could not help remarking that as the congregation left they gathered into little knots of twos and threes to discuss the subject of the archbishop's sermon, which denounced more vehemently than ever the doctrine taught by Arius. It had been the common topic of conversation in Alexandria for months now. Slaves at the fruit-stalls, merchants meeting to talk over the price of wheat and figs, as well as the parabolani with their deacons, were all discussing the same abstruse subject—the beginning of the being of Christ: whether He, like the Father, was from all eternity, or whether, as Arius declared, He was inferior to the Father—not co-eternal or co-equal.

EVINCED: *clearly showed*
ABSTRUSE: *hard to understand*

This was the question agitating Alexandrian society and the whole Christian Church at large, and the ever-watchful foes—the Jews and the worshipers of the fallen gods—were eagerly watching for an opportunity to throw discredit upon either party or both parties in this strife.

It was soon understood that the emperor's letter had not pleased the patriarch, Alexander, and Quadratus heard from his friend Athanasius that Constantine had arrogated to himself the power of dictating to the archbishop as to the expediency of recalling Arius and dropping this discussion.

"It is as I feared," said the young deacon; "we are to yield our liberty as the price of imperial patronage, and I, in my poor person, will oppose it. Nothing can compensate for the loss of this," he went on; "better be persecuted than patronized at the price of liberty."

Many of the deacons and presbyters gave expression to even more intemperate language than this, and the parabolani taking up the cause still more warmly, Alexandria was soon in a state of profound agitation. It might, however, have passed over quietly enough but for the sneering remarks of some Jews concerning the cowardice of Christians in grumbling at the emperor and yet bowing down to his effigy, for Alexandria, in her gratitude, had raised a statue to the honor of Constantine.

ARROGATED: *presumptuously claimed*
INTEMPERATE: *uncontrolled*
EFFIGY: *image*

This sneer was all that was needed to set in a blaze the already inflamed passions of the mob, and the next moment the statue was hurled from its pedestal, and the Jews had cried, "Traitors and incendiaries," and were fiercely contending for the fragments of the broken marble.

The news of this disturbance spread quickly, and despite the arrival of the prefect, Appicatus, upon the scene, Jews and Christians were soon engaged in a fierce struggle—not now for the possession of a few broken pieces of marble, but for a whole quarter of a city. It was no hand to hand combat now, but monks and citizens of all grades had armed themselves with the first missiles that came to hand to fight against their Jewish adversaries, not hesitating to enter the houses and shops, and help themselves to what they wanted. Of course, the Jews were not slow to follow this initiative, and when the owners resisted they were assailed, and in many cases the houses set on fire, amid shouts and screams of terror and triumph. The worshipers of Serapis and the old Greek deities were not one whit behind their Jewish coadjutors, and urged on the mob with cries of, "Death to the Christian traitors! death to these murdering monks!" for many of these anchorites of the desert had come to the city just now and were foremost in the fray, though it was more in the way of parrying blows than striking them. On the mob rushed, spreading consternation wherever they appeared,

INCENDIARIES: *those who stir up strife*
ONE WHIT: *one bit*
COADJUTORS: *assistants*

until, at last, the retired quarter where Quadratus and his mother were living was itself invaded.

The young soldier had only just assured her that there was little fear of the rioters reaching them, when the mob was heard entering the street, and the next minute half a dozen slaves ran into the inner court, where they were sitting in an agony of terror. "Hush, hush, ye will frighten my mother," said Quadratus.

But the brave old lady assured him she was not alarmed, although she grew pale as another shout reached her from the mob outside. "This is not the first riot I have seen in our streets," she said, rising as she spoke. "I will go to Placidia, my Quadratus, and do thou keep guard if it be needful."

But before going to the door Quadratus led his mother toward the tower-stairs, and it was well he did so, for before she had mounted half a dozen steps she fainted in his arms, and he carried her back to the open court at once and dispatched one of the female slaves to summon his sister.

Placidia was not long in obeying the summons, and, with a hasty assurance that there was nothing to fear, Quadratus rushed to the entrance gates just in time to see them forced open by a party of Jews. Quadratus was unarmed, but he fought manfully and tried to rouse the courage of the slaves to help him, but the sight of half a dozen Jews fighting with vine-stocks, stones, and sticks indiscriminately, was too much for them

ANCHORITES: *hermits*
CONSTERNATION: *sudden alarm and dismay*
VINE-STOCKS: *vine-stems*

and they fled, leaving Quadratus bruised, bleeding, almost dead, in a recess where his enemies had pushed him while they made their way into the house.

On they rushed, furious with passion, maddened with the delay at the gates, breaking and destroying all that came before them, until the inner court was reached, and there they paused for a moment at the sight of the helpless nun and the white-haired old lady, still lying on the cushions where her son had placed her. Only for a moment did they pause in their work of destruction, and then one of them seized Placidia by the wrist and hurried her away; but no one dared to touch the still silent form of the old lady, and they went out leaving her undisturbed in her dreamless sleep.

When Quadratus recovered consciousness the noise of the tumult was dying away in the distance, and after a great effort he managed to crawl out of the friendly recess which had been the means of saving his life, and dragged his bruised, bleeding limbs through the vestibule to the inner court, where he saw his mother still lying apparently in undisturbed repose, although vases, urns, and flowers had been torn from their places and dashed to pieces all around.

"Thank God they have not injured her!" he said, half-aloud, as he ventured to call, in a feeble voice, "Mother, Mother!" But no answer came to his call, and, in some alarm, he laid his hand upon her forehead. Alas! that was as cold as the marble

REPOSE: *sleep*

pillar near which she lay, and looking then more closely at the set, rigid features, he saw that she was dead! With a bitter cry of anguish he flung himself beside her, and for a few minutes gave himself up to the unrestrained indulgence of his grief. Then, suddenly recollecting that he had left Placidia beside her, he turned to look for his sister, but she was nowhere to be seen; and some of the slaves having now ventured to creep out of their hiding-places, he dispatched several in search of her.

But they soon returned with the alarming intelligence that she was nowhere to be found. Every room in the house had been searched, but no trace of her could be discovered; and the only hope Quadratus had was, that she had gone to Melissa's for assistance, or in search of him.

This hope, however, was soon dispelled, for Lucullus himself came in a few minutes' afterward to inquire how they had fared, for the guards, or stationaries, as they were called, had quelled the disturbance at last.

"Placidia hath told thee all, hath she not?" asked Quadratus, with a slight groan.

"I have not seen Placidia, but I can see the miscreants have done a good deal of mischief. Art thou hurt?" suddenly asked Lucullus, noticing for the first time his torn, disordered dress and bleeding hands.

"A little, not much," answered Quadratus faintly, and then added, "But my mother, Lucullus—the strife hath killed her."

QUELLED: *quieted*
MISCREANTS: *evildoers*

"Killed her!" exclaimed Lucullus, stooping to look closer at the pale, set features. Quadratus did not hear his brother-in-law's next exclamation, for he had fainted; and while he was still unconscious, Lucullus had him placed on a mattress and carried to his own house, that Melissa might nurse him under the doctor's directions, while at the same time he ordered the slaves to remove as far as possible all traces of the riot, and prepare the body of their mistress for the funeral.

His next care was to make further inquiries for Placidia among the neighboring houses, but no one had seen the young nun, and at last the funeral took place without any tidings being obtained as to her hiding-place. One hope alone remained to her anxious friends now, and that was that she had escaped and gone to Orestes in the desert. She had long been anxious to leave her home and devote herself to an eremitic life they knew, and at length Quadratus determined to ascertain this fact by going himself to the *laura*, or hermits' colony, where his brother lived, as soon as he was able to travel.

This mission Athanasius promised to aid by obtaining for him a letter from the patriarch to the abbot of the colony; but at the same time he warned him not to attempt to remove Placidia from her retirement if he found her, and this Quadratus readily promised, as his sole anxiety now was to be certain that she had escaped a fate worse than death

EREMITIC LIFE: *hermit-like life at a convent*

to one brought up as Placidia had been. To divert
his mind from this all-engrossing anxiety as to his
sister's fate, the young deacon then told him of the
progress of public affairs in Alexandria. Hosius
had returned to Byzantium, having effected nothing by his visit, for Alexander and his clergy were
more than ever determined to hold aloof from
Arius. "His doctrine hath done mischief enough
already," went on Athanasius; "for he would have
men believe that the Son of God was a man of like
passions as ourselves, and effectually deprive us of
the due reverence we ought to feel in approaching
Him, so that it behooves every man now to preach
and teach His power and godhead fully, and without compromise."

Little did Athanasius suspect that in his zeal
to uphold the honor and power of the Lord Jesus
Christ he was so overlooking His love and tenderness that many a sensitive, repentant soul was
growing afraid to approach Him—was losing sight
of Him as a Saviour who could be touched with a
feeling of their infirmities, and began to regard
Him as a Judge who was removed from them to an
infinite distance, where in majesty and glory He
reigned supreme, all but indifferent to the struggles and efforts of poor, frail, erring mortals, who
knelt before Him.

It was not what Alexander or his true and devout
young deacon meant to teach, but it was what men
and women had begun to deduce from it; and this

feeling, now arising in so many earnest, inquiring minds, laid the foundation of one of the grossest errors into which the Church afterward fell.

This danger, however, was not apprehended at that time; but Quadratus had foreseen that his sister's plan of retaining the old statues in her household and calling them by Christian names might be a prolific source of misconception by and by, and he mentioned the matter to Athanasius one day, for he knew the young deacon must have noticed this.

He shook his head gravely in reply. "I know not what to think about it," he said; "many, like Melissa, are anxious to win new converts by any and all means; and concessions are thus made, and old customs retained, that would be better discontinued."

"The danger is not for the present generation, perhaps," said Quadratus; "but it is possible, I think, that these statues, renamed though they are, may be the cause of a revival of another form of idolatry."

"It were better, certainly, if they were put away, and the old simplicity retained in all things;" and Athanasius sighed as he reflected that this simplicity was passing away, not only in the matter of domestic and household arrangements, but in the conduct of public worship in the churches.

"We are fallen upon evil times, I fear, in spite of all this seeming prosperity," said Quadratus, with a half-drawn sigh.

GROSSEST: *most extreme*
APPREHENDED: *understood*

"Nay, nay, say not so," interrupted Athanasius quickly. "The Church Catholic is rising into power —putting on her glorious apparel to conquer the nations of the world for our God."

"But she must beware, lest the world, having failed to crush her by its terrors, should now soothe her into sloth and forgetfulness by its blandishments," said Quadratus.

"Sloth and forgetfulness," repeated Athanasius, in a half-offended tone. "Have we been slothful or forgetful in this dispute with Arius?" he asked.

"Nay, it was of myself rather than of thee I was thinking, for it is not so easy to be watchful and prayerful now as in the days of persecution," said the soldier, who during his illness had had time to review the latter years of his life passed in the eager bustle of the camp and court, and by no means conducive to a very regular or devout life.

Quadratus had always been regarded, and thought himself, a very excellent Christian, but he began to see now that a good deal of what was once deep religious life to him had now drifted into a mere formalism—a dead shell—the life from which had departed.

"The world is dangerous—is alluring," assented Athanasius, "and canst thou wonder that so many fly from it to an undisturbed life of prayer and meditation in the desert, where they can serve God undisturbed by the cares and pleasures, pomps and ambitions, of the world, which is still lying in wickedness."

BLANDISHMENTS: *flatteries and enticements*
POMPS: *showy displays*

"And yet it was the world lying in wickedness that God loved and Christ came to redeem," said Quadratus thoughtfully.

Athanasius did not notice the interruption. "Could there be a stronger protest against the luxury and sensuality of this age than the voluntary giving up of all social ties, all home joys, all civilized society, for a life of toil, and prayer, and meditation, alone in the desert or in some lonely *laura*," he said, as though he would persuade the soldier to embrace this eremitic life for himself.

"It is a protest, as thou sayest, Athanasius, and it gives an honor and dignity to common everyday toil; but still, self-denying as these men and women are, would it not be better for the world and for themselves to remain in their appointed stations, laboring still, and fighting against the temptations by which they are surrounded instead of flying from them, which to me savors of cowardice."

"Nay, nay, my Quadratus, wait until thou hast seen our monks of Nitria before thou dost accuse them of cowardice," said Athanasius, rising as he spoke, for he saw there was little chance of agreement between them on this topic at present, and so he wisely withdrew.

SAVORS: *smells*

Chapter V

A Fruitless Search

IT was arranged that not only Quadratus but Melissa and little Alypus, with half a dozen household slaves to attend upon them, should go by barge from Alexandria up the Nile, to the nearest point from whence Orestes could be reached, by which time Quadratus would so far have recovered his strength as to be able to perform this part of his journey on foot if he could not obtain any conveyance. A large store of provisions was taken on board, which, with fresh supplies of fruit and fish obtained at the villages along the banks, allowed them to pursue their voyage in a very leisurely fashion, which suited the rowers quite as well as it did Melissa. Over the after part of the elegant gilded barge was spread an ornamented awning under which some mattresses and a pile of cushions were laid, and here the lady could lounge or play with her little boy all day or talk to Quadratus, who preferred to sit outside and see what was passing around him, and where she could sleep comfortably at night.

CONVEYANCE: *transportation*

"We shall see nothing up this miserable canal," said Melissa with a sigh, as she waved her fan of peacock's feathers, and adjusted her thin silk robe in more graceful folds. Melissa had not thought much about this matter of dress at one time, but she was a fashionable lady now, and it engrossed a good deal of her attention. A heavy gold cross was suspended from her neck, and a small roll of parchment, set and clasped with jewels, hung from her girdle, but it was rarely opened, as Quadratus noticed, and little Alypus was left almost entirely to the care of the slaves.

Before the first week was over Melissa began to complain of the monotony of their voyage. "There is nothing to see but these high mud banks and a waterwheel here and there," she grumbled.

"I am afraid we shall have to depend upon each other a good deal for diversion," said Quadratus, "unless thou dost like watching the reflection of the skies in the waters below."

Melissa uttered an exclamation of disgust. "I am tired of everything there is to be seen here," she said with a yawn.

"Alypus finds plenty of amusement," said her brother, as the child came running toward him to announce some fresh discovery he had made.

"There is another raft of jars going to be sold," he lisped as one of these came floating past. "I wonder whether they are going to our market."

"Perhaps they are," said Quadratus; "but look, there are some monks fishing from that boat in

GIRDLE: *belt*

the bay. I wonder whether Orestes is still fond of fishing." This last remark was addressed to his sister rather than to the child.

"I wish Orestes would settle the question concerning his share of the property," said Melissa testily.

"I thought it was settled—that as he had given up all share in the active business of life the Church should receive all that of right became his."

Melissa pouted. "The Church is growing enormously rich, I should think, there are so often bequests of land, money, houses, and jewels left to it now."

"Melissa, dost thou grudge the Church these riches?" asked her brother.

The lady looked confused, and murmured something about her share being small and her private expenses heavy, but before she could say anything openly Quadratus spoke again.

"Think of the heavy burden the Church hath to sustain in the care of all the poor and sick," he said; "if it were not for this gracious law of the emperor, which empowers the Church to receive such gifts, they could not be fed and clothed."

"Then the State would have to look after them," said Melissa. "Lucullus says this was just a clever trick of Constantine to get rid of a troublesome burden, and an easy way of providing for it, by which he got rid of all the expense and responsibility."

Quadratus looked shocked. He had never seen

TESTILY: *irritably*

his sister in this mood before, and he was at a loss to understand it. To turn the conversation, therefore, he spoke of Placidia, and her desire to enter upon a life of poverty and privation.

"I could never endure it, I am sure," said Melissa; "and I think thou hadst better persuade her to return with thee."

"We are not yet sure of finding her," said Quadratus with an anxious sigh as a long line of palm-leaf huts came into view at a short distance from the bank of the river, and where it was just possible his sister had found shelter while on her way to the more distant *laura*.

"Quadratus, what wilt thou do if Orestes hath not heard of her?" asked Melissa, rousing herself from her lethargy.

The soldier shook his head. "It is my last hope for her, Melissa," he said, "and I cannot contemplate the failure of that, for the only other alternative is too dreadful to think of."

"What is it?" asked Melissa anxiously.

"Hast thou not thought that these Jews, in their grasping love of money and hatred of all Christians, might sell our sister?" said Quadratus in a lower tone.

"Sell her! sell our Placidia!" gasped Melissa in horror. "What dost thou mean?"

"That I fear it may be so—that it is quite possible they may sell Placidia in one of the European slave-markets," said the soldier, trying to hide his emotion.

PRIVATION: *a lack of comforts and necessities*
LETHARGY: *drowsiness*

Melissa forgot her apathy and her indolent airs now. "Placidia a slave!" she gasped. "O, Quadratus, save her—save my poor little Placidia from such a cruel fate!"

"I will if it be possible! Hush, hush, Melissa, do not cry; it may be that she hath gone to Orestes or to some company of nuns here in the desert."

"Thou wilt find her if it is so; and if not—O, my brother—"

"Nay, nay, do not think the case so hopeless. If the worst hath happened Lucullus may yet discover her, for he hath sent to Rome and Byzantium, offering a large ransom for her."

"Then Lucullus feared this likewise," said Melissa.

"We feared it might be possible; but I still hope she escaped to the desert. Thou wilt be brave, Melissa, and let me leave the boat tomorrow to inquire at some of the convents; otherwise, we may pass on and never discover her."

"Could I not go with thee?" asked the lady.

"It would so sorely hinder me that I fear we should never find her, for thou knowest if thou wert to appear near a *laura* all the monks would leave it." The soldier smiled at the thought of a daintily dressed lady, like Melissa, invading the monk's seclusion, and wondered what Orestes would say when he saw her approaching.

"I suppose I should hinder thee," said Melissa with a sigh; "but thou wilt come back to me in a day or two?"

APATHY: *lack of emotion*
INDOLENT: *lazy*

"I think my promise had better be conditional. Thou shalt go on as far as Thebes, and wait there one day for me; if possible, I will join thee there; but, if I should not come, do not stay longer, or Lucullus will grow anxious. I will return to Alexandria as speedily as possible; but I know not what hinderances there may be in the way of finding Placidia, even if she should be in the desert."

"Thou thinkest thou will find her, dost thou not?" said Melissa, anxious for the smallest hope concerning her sister.

"Yes, I pray she may have gone to Orestes; but, my Melissa, thou must not forget she is in God's hands wherever she may be," said Quadratus tenderly. "He knoweth our anxiety, and her unfitness for toil and hardship; for He knoweth our frame, and the Lord Christ can sympathize with her as well as with us, and—"

"But—but dost thou think the Lord Christ does sympathize with our little sorrows and cares now? He did with His disciples, of course, but He is so great, and high, and holy now, I feel afraid to go to Him as—as our father used," said Melissa in a hesitating tone.

"Afraid, my sister!" repeated Quadratus.

"Yes; in the eternal majesty and glory where He hath dwelt from all eternity, how can such poor, unworthy prayers as mine reach Him," and Melissa almost shivered as she spoke.

In a moment Quadratus seemed to understand

her difficulty, and how it had arisen. "The Lord
Christ seems to have removed so much farther off
now than in the old days of trouble and persecution, is not that it, Melissa?" he asked.

"Ah, those old days! they were happy days,
Quadratus, in spite of the persecution. The Lord
Christ seemed to be a real, personal friend to
each one of them. I was not so old as Placidia is
now, but I can remember I never felt afraid to go
to Him any more than I was of confessing a fault
to my mother. How is it—what makes the difference?" she asked.

"My sister, be sure of this, the difference is not in
Him but in thee. He has not moved further from
thee, but thou dost care less to live near Him. That
is the chief reason. But I think there is also another. Our holy patriarch, in his care and anxiety
lest people should fall into the old error of saying
there be gods many and lords many—in his devout
desire that the Lord Christ should be duly honored and reverenced—for fear they should have
any leaning toward this Arianism that now threat-
ens to divide the Church—has of late preached and
taught almost exclusively the power and majesty,
and honor and glory of the Lord Christ; and so
by degrees people are beginning to lose the consciousness of His tenderness, sympathy, and love,
and placed Him far away from them as it seems;
but thou must remember it is only in *seeming*,
Melissa, for He is 'the same yesterday, today, and

forever.'[1] 'For we have not an high priest which cannot be touched with the feeling of our infirmities; but was in all points tempted like as we are, yet without sin.'[2] Try to think of this, Melissa, as well as the power and glory of Christ, and then He will not be so far off," said Quadratus as he concluded.

But after he had left the boat and taken the road leading to the nearest monastery his thoughts went back to this conversation, and he wondered whether others as well as Melissa had began to feel that Christ was afar off from them now. "It is the natural recoil from the teaching of Arius, I suppose, and yet there may be a danger in this—it may be pushed too far until men and women are afraid to approach the Friend of sinners." The possibility that this recoil could push the Saviour from His place, as the mediator between God and man, Quadratus never once glanced at any more than Athanasius or Alexander. Could they have foreseen the practical effect of their insistence upon this one-sided view of the Lord's character and attributes, they would, with all the energy and faithfulness of their devout and earnest souls, have combated the slightest approach to a deification of the Lord's mother, which was the actual outcome of this total forgetfulness of His humanity. He was still thinking of this and the disturbed state of the Church of Alexandria, when he came upon a little colony of huts, and a monk at once

---

[1] HEBREWS 13:8   [2] HEBREWS 4:15

DEIFICATION: *making a god*

came forward to proffer what hospitality he had at command upon the stranger.

Maize and millet, with fish as an occasional dainty, was quite sufficient for the brotherhood, but they had some dried meat and a few small skins of wine for the refection of strangers, and this was pressed upon the soldier before he had stated the errand upon which he had come.

Isolated as these men were, news from the outer world rarely reached them, and so the tidings Quadratus brought from Alexandria were welcome indeed, and the abbot at once dispatched two of the brothers to make inquiries at the neighboring monasteries and convents concerning Placidia, while the soldier rested and refreshed himself preparatory to resuming his journey, for he was still two days' travel from the *laura* where Orestes presided.

No tidings of Placidia could be gained by the monks, and so Quadratus set off on his journey through the desert, guided by his hosts which direction to take so as to call upon each little colony of hermits as he passed, for they were dotted here and there, like oases in the boundless expanse of the arid, sandy waste, that stretched on and on to an almost limitless extent as it seemed to Quadratus.

The *laura* over which his brother presided as abbot was reached at last, and his heart beat high with hope that tidings of Placidia would be gained at last.

PROFFER: *offer*
AT COMMAND: *at his disposal*
REFECTION: *refreshment*

The palm-leaf huts were built under the shadow of a wall of crags, and here, in the midst of the desert, they had created a little oasis; for with infinite labor they had carried up from the banks of the Nile sufficient earth to plant a garden, where they grew maize, millet, and pulse, which sufficed for their few wants; and for clothing a ragged sheepskin, secured by a leathern girdle, was all they needed and all thcy wore; and to obtain these, and send something to those poorer than themselves, each brother worked diligently, weaving palm-leaf mats or baskets when not engaged upon the garden or at prayers. And hither had come men of whom the world was not worthy—earnest souls, who had grown sick of the rottenness and corruption that pervaded all ranks of society, and who, longing for closer and nearer communion with God, sought it by flying from their fellows and hiding themselves even from their own families. There was one thing, however, they did not forget, and that was the blessing of the curse: "In the sweat of thy face shalt thou eat bread."[1] In the world they had fled from, work was despised and shunned; but there the fathers of agriculture and the custodians of literature gave a new law to the world, and dignified labor by working with their might at whatsoever their hand found to do. They were no drones, these early monkish fathers, and if they made the mistake of flying from those made, like themselves, in the image of God—and

---

[1] GENESIS 3:19

PULSE: *beans and lentils*

DRONES: *those who do mindless, menial work*

whom the common Father would have had them serve and recognized the service as done unto Himself—we cannot feel greatly surprised, for men had ceased to be men and become monsters. The giant evil that had well-nigh crushed the Church now threatened to debase it, and holiness, purity, and virtue could only be found in that world which these men had set themselves to contemplate and prepare themselves for, to the total exclusion of this.

When Quadratus reached the *laura* and asked for Brother Orestes he was shown at once to his rude hut, and while one brother went to fetch him from the garden in which he was working, another placed before the soldier a bunch of dried dates and some palm wine; but Quadratus was too anxious about his sister to eat or drink, and when he saw his brother, in his ragged sheepskin, slowly approaching, he went out to meet him.

"My brother, dost thou not know me—thy brother in the flesh, Quadratus?" he asked.

The long, gaunt, bony arm was raised, and he placed his sun-browned horny hand over his eyes to screen them a little from the sun's rays as he said, slowly, "Thou art Quadratus, from Alexandria!"

"Yes, I came from Alexandria in search of our sister, Placidia. Hast thou seen her, Orestes?"

"Seen Placidia, my sister? Nay, thou knowest her holy desire to dwell in the desert was opposed by

DEBASE IT: *bring it low*

all her friends in the flesh, how then should I see her."

For a moment Quadratus was too much agitated to reply; but when they reached the tent he drew forth the patriarch's letter, and afterward told Orestes of the riot, his mother's death, and Placidia's mysterious disappearance.

For a moment Orestes too seemed agitated, but he quickly subdued his emotion, as being too carnal for a monk's indulgence, and said, though still with a slight tremor in his voice, "The sin of these her friends hath fallen heavily upon them, and doubtless they feel it as a sore judgment of the Lord to have her thus removed."

"Nay, it is not for ourselves, but for her, we grieve. Think, Orestes, if she hath not escaped to the desert, what her fate may be."

"The Lord hath removed her, I say, and He knows how to take care of His own," said the monk calmly; and to all Quadratus' anxious fears he returned the same answer—not that he did not care for Placidia's fate, but he devoutly believed in miracles still being performed, and in his own mind he was sure Placidia had been the subject of one, and was now miraculously removed from the world to some lonely *laura*.

CARNAL: *worldly*

QUADRATUS FINDS ORESTES

Chapter VI

At Nicæa

QUADRATUS was by no means so sure that Placidia had been removed from Alexandria by heavenly intervention as his brother. He feared that motives only too earthly and mercenary had led to her mysterious disappearance, but all his fears failed to arouse any alarm in Orestes. She was in God's hands, he said, and He could guard His own, a truth the soldier did not attempt to contradict, only he believed in the use of ordinary methods to ascertain her situation, while Orestes trusted implicitly in the miraculous, and looked upon all human agency as savoring of a want of faith; so that Quadratus received no encouragement from him to push his researches further. Having been already longer than he anticipated, he resolved to return to Alexandria with all speed, lest dispatches should have arrived from Byzantium summoning him to return.

He would fain have lingered among the titanic ruins of the old world cities with which this

IMPLICITLY: *unquestioningly*
AGENCY: *actions, methods*
TITANIC: *enormous*

portion of Egypt was studded, but he had to be content with a passing glimpse of these as he glided down the Nile in his flat-bottomed boat, for Melissa had returned and almost reached Alexandria again by this time.

It was well he had not lingered longer in the desert, for on reaching the city he was met with the startling news of tidings having reached Alexandria that Lycinius, the last of the Cæsars who ruled jointly with Constantine, had again taken up arms against his brother-in-law and colleague, and that another war was impending.

"I am not greatly surprised," said Quadratus, "for he hateth the Christians, it is well-known, and would commence another persecution if he only had the power. I must hasten to Byzantium with all speed," he added, "for although the war with the Goths was only just over when I came here, our soldiers will be ready enough to strike a blow at this last enemy of the Church."

"The last enemy!" repeated Lucullus with something of a smile. "Nay, nay, Lycinius is by no means the last enemy; and if we are to have such riots as this we have had lately, we had better return to the old gods and the games of the arena again, for it injures trade and brings discredit upon our city to have such disturbances."

"But thou canst not charge the Christians with this riot," said Quadratus; "the Jews and the followers of the old gods were the chief aggressors, and—"

IMPENDING: *about to happen*
PROSECUTE: *continue*

"But this Christianity was the cause," said Lucullus quickly, "and it is damaging trade."

Anxious to turn the conversation, Quadratus asked when the next vessel would sail for Byzantium, and on hearing that one would leave the following day he determined to go by that, and charged Lucullus still to prosecute his inquiries concerning Placidia, as he was by no means so sure that she had died as Melissa was, or that she had found an asylum in the desert as Orestes supposed.

By the time Quadratus had reached Byzantium the army, led by Constantine himself, was ready to take the field, and the guard of the labarum had already been summoned to rally round the sacred banner, that should once more lead them on to victory. These fifty guards, whose duty it was to march with the ensign at the head of the troops and lead them on the foremost in the battle, were by everybody considered invulnerable; and officers and men pressed on in the rear of the sacred shadow of that long pike with its transversal beam and silken veil which hung from the crosspiece, and which was inwrought with the images of the emperor and his family, and surmounted by a cross of gold, which might be seen gleaming above all surrounding objects.

Every soldier had a cross emblazoned upon his shield, for by this had their emperor conquered in every battle; and it had been revealed to him in a miraculous vision as a weapon and defense

ASYLUM: *a place of refuge*
INVULNERABLE: *impossible to defeat*

by which he should conquer—at least that was his own account of its adoption, and miracles were readily credited in those days. But there were many, doubtless, who thought Constantine's victories might be accounted for by his energy, promptitude, and the good discipline of his army; and thought him a far-seeing politician, in patronizing this rising power of Christianity which his predecessors had tried in vain to crush out.

With hymns and shouts of "Alleluia" the well-disciplined troops marched forth once more—not this time against Goths and barbarians but brothers and comrades-in-arms, for they had once fought side by side against a common foe. But the army of Lycinius had grown indolent and self-indulgent from a long peace, and when at length they met on the plains of Adrianople, a few miles from Byzantium—Christian against pagan—the battle was a decisive one. The army of Lycinius was completely routed, and he himself was killed afterward—a murder that must always stain the memory of Constantine.

This war was not a long one, and it left Constantine sole master of the vast Roman Empire, in gratitude for which he now ordered that many of the old temples of the gods, which of course belonged to the State, should be handed over to the Christians, as that was now the national religion.

But the emperor's troubles were not quite at an end. A rebellion broke out in his favored city

PROMPTITUDE: *good timing*
PREDECESSORS: *those who held the position before him*
ROUTED: *defeated and scattered*

of Byzantium, and before it could be quelled the old town was completely destroyed. The situation of this ancient city was too favorable, however, to be deserted, for it commanded an important trade between the east and west; and the only half-subdued empire of the East could be awed into submission by the emperor fixing upon this as his capital, while, at the same time, he could have an eye upon Rome, which was now too effete to cause him much anxiety, although it retained something of its old form of a senate.

The ruins were, therefore, quickly cleared away, and treasures of marble, and porphyry statues and columns, were soon brought from all parts of the empire to build and embellish a city worthy of the first Christian emperor, and to be called after his name.

Peace having now been restored to the world at large, Constantine resolved to make another effort toward restoring peace to the Church by the calling of a general council of bishops, to meet at Nicæa, in Nicomedia, during the summer of this year, 325, and Quadratus began to look forward to this, as he would hear of his friends in Alexandria from the bishop and the deacons who would accompany him.

Every town and village in the empire was busy with festive preparations this spring, for Constantine would celebrate his victory over Lycinius, and it was likewise customary for the Roman

EFFETE: *weak, worn-out*
EMBELLISH: *make beautiful, decorate*

emperors to observe each tenth year of their reign as a season of rejoicing, and this being the twentieth year of Constantine's reign, and, moreover, the first general council of the Church which had met since the time of the apostles, everybody was looking forward with eager anticipation to the arrival of the visitors in the little town of Nicæa, nestling at the foot of the hills of Nicomedia.

Constantine was anxious to do his guests all honor, and came here himself first to see that his palace was in complete order, and that the stadium, where the assembly would first meet, was ready to receive them; and he was well-pleased to see that every portico along the straight streets of the square-built town had been cleaned and furbished, as well as every heathen device removed from the stadium. Quadratus was left behind when Constantine went back to see that all his arrangements for the comfort of his expected guests were duly carried out, and that each bishop might have the attendance of three slaves if they had not brought their own with them.

The first to arrive were two from Upper Egypt, Paphnutius and Potamon, and Quadratus stepped forward to greet them as they alighted from their mules. No daintily-dressed bishops were these, for more than half their lives had been spent as hermits in the desert, whither they had been driven by the last severe persecution under Diocletian, and they still wore the rough sheepskin cloak

FURBISHED: *repaired*
UNKEMPT: *uncombed*
TOILETS: *grooming and dressing*

without sleeves, and their hair and beards were an
unkempt, tangled mass. But it was not this that
made Quadratus start from them with such a look
of horror and the next minute fall upon his knees
and reverently kiss the edge of their dirty sheepskin cloaks, for he had been used to see such neglected toilets very often in the desert, but never
before had he met with any so disfigured as these
two bishops, for the right eye of each had been
dug out and the cavity all round seared with a red-
hot iron. In addition to this Paphnutius was lame,
having had his left leg hamstrung in the same persecution.

No wonder the people came out, not only
to look at but to weep over and almost worship
the two old men who had so bravely suffered for
Christ, as they sat under the shadow of the porticoes near the stadium and talked over this world's
wonder—the gathering of a council of bishops
under the presidency of a Roman emperor.

Each day brought a fresh arrival now, and one
of the earliest, as he was also the first in dignity,
was Custathius, of Antioch—the "City of God" as
it was usually called. With him came the Bishop
of Cæsarea, Eusebius, the interpreter, and chap-
lain of Constantine, and to whom, as the father of
ecclesiastical history, we are indebted for the account of this council. Eusebius, however, was shy
of the Egyptian bishops, and, in spite of their being confessors, sought the company of the more

ECCLESIASTICAL: *church*
CONFESSORS: *those who have confessed, or acknowledged,*
their faith in God despite persecution

polite and learned, and it began to be whispered that he had failed in the hour of trial, and had escaped a like mutilation by sacrificing to the popular gods.

But he was high in the emperor's favor now, and could afford to smile at the reverence with which some of the fruit-sellers and market-women treasured a stray scrap of their old garments as some precious relic, for he was sought by each of the new arrivals, who was anxious to learn the bent of the emperor's mind on the subject in dispute.

Paphnutius, however, was not the only one who bore in his body "the marks of the Lord Jesus."[1] Paul of Neocæsarea had both hands paralyzed, from the fingers being scorched with hot irons; and of the three hundred and eighteen who at length assembled, there were scarcely fifty who were not partially maimed, halt, or blind, from the sufferings they had endured in the cause of their Master.

With a council composed of such men, was it likely that any doctrine touching the honor of their Master would be allowed to receive their assent, however anxious Constantine might be to secure peace?

Arius himself, with his friend Eusebius, of Nicomedia, was one of the last to arrive; but one glance at the man was sufficient to see that he was as thoroughly in earnest as any of his opponents, and as little likely to concede to the emperor's views if

---

[1] GALATIANS 6:17
RELIC: *holy object*
HALT: *lame*

they involved a giving up of his opinions. There were others besides the Bishop of Nicomedia who favored him, and he would stand in the midst of this little crowd of disciples and pour out a torrent of fiery eloquence in support of his views that threatened to bear down all opposition. Towering above the tallest of these, and swaying his thin, emaciated body backward and forward, while his face lighted sometimes with a smile of rare sweetness and gentleness, or contracted by a frown of fierce denunciation, he alternately persuaded or threatened his hearers, sometimes growing so enthusiastic as to indulge in a frenzied dance, that made many not accustomed to him suppose he was mad.

Quadratus began to fear that some accident must have befallen the Bishop of Alexandria and his party. He was the chief opponent to Arius, and many wondered how he would meet his former presbyter and deacon, for these good men were only human after all, and many of them nursed private quarrels and grudges against each other, and were as eager to tell of each other's faults and failings as the rest of mankind.

Alexander, with his chief deacon, Athanasius, and their attendant slaves, reached the city at last, after a perilous voyage by sea and a wearisome journey by land. Alexander himself, now very aged, and growing more feeble every month, was quite exhausted, and only his friend Hosius, of

ELOQUENCE: *skillful and persuasive speaking*
EMACIATED: *wasted away*
DENUNCIATION: *condemnation*

Cordova, was admitted to his presence for several days.

At length the whole number invited having either arrived or sent representatives, they were gathered together in the stadium for their first formal meeting, to seek the blessing of God upon their deliberations, after which they met in the porticoes, or in the gardens on the shore of the little lake, and waited the coming of the emperor, who was to open the council in person. Constantine wisely delayed his arrival for some days, to allow these men of such varied attainments and experience to meet each other in open, friendly, informal discussion, and state their own peculiar views concerning this matter that threatened to destroy the peace of the Church. Of course each had his own peculiar reason for assent or dissent from Arius' doctrine, and, looked at from so many different standpoints, it bore so many different shades that it was even possible that instead of making peace this council might make matters worse unless its affairs were wisely managed; and when Quadratus saw how fierce these disputants were—each for his own view of the subject being right, and the only right one—he began to despair of peace and harmony ever being evolved out of such discordant elements.

"I would rather fight ten battles than preside at a council of bishops," he exclaimed one day half-aloud—loud enough for one of them to hear him

TEUTONS: *Germanic peoples*
THOR AND ODIN: *Norse gods*

speak, but who as yet had taken no very active part in the discussion, although if his mental powers bore any resemblance to his physical frame he would bear down all before him, for he was a perfect giant. He laughed aloud as he saw the young soldier's look of perplexity, but he could not speak a word of Greek, and only the Latin tongue imperfectly, for he was a Goth—perhaps the first among the Teutons who had ever risen to the dignity of being a servant of God.

Finding Quadratus could converse a little in his own barbarian tongue, the giant bishop, Theophilus, entered into a conversation with him concerning his hopes of one of his deacons, Ulphilas, becoming a missionary to the wild tribes of his countrymen in the north. Theophilus had little sympathy, it seemed, with the abstruse subject they had met to decide either one way or the other. He was anxious to win his countrymen from the worship of Thor and Odin to the service of Jesus Christ, and to point out to them that the Asgard they dreamed of, and hoped to find in the countries of the South, was not all a dream, but that there was a kingdom where the spirits of just men made perfect would dwell with God forever—a kingdom "not made with hands, eternal in the heavens."[1]

One day a party of learned prelates were growing quite warm over the disputed subject, and Theophilus and Quadratus proportionally

---

[1] II CORINTHIANS 5:1
ASGARD: *the capital city of the gods in Norse mythology*
PRELATES: *high church officials*

weary, when a simple-minded hermit, who had drawn near to hear what was said, suddenly rose to his feet and exclaimed, "Christ and the apostles left us not a system of logic, but a naked truth, to be guarded by faith and good works!" These words were not without effect on the angry bishops, and by degrees they grew more calm, and soon learned to see that the difference in the views held by them and many of their seeming opponents only existed in form and the use of words and not in actual fact, and thus many opposing elements were drawn together before the emperor came to open the council.

Chapter VII

The First Council

THE arrival of the emperor at his temporary
palace of Nicæa put an end to the prelimi-
nary meetings of the bishops, and they were sum-
moned to meet in the large central hall of the palace, where chairs had been placed for the bishops,
and a seat behind each for his attendant presbyter
or deacon. Many of them had never yet seen the
emperor, and there were a few minutes of anxious
suspense before the guards approached who were
to herald his coming. No heathen, however high
his rank might be, was allowed to enter the presence of these men of God; but Quadratus and a
few of his Christian friends took their place at the
back of the raised gilt chair which had been placed
at the upper end for the emperor, and the next
moment a cursor raised a torch at the entrance,
on which all the bishops rose to receive the emperor.

Constantine was of majestic height and bearing, with a handsome face of mingled sweetness
and fierceness, that betokened his character most

CURSOR: *herald*
BETOKENED: *showed*

clearly. His long flowing robe of imperial purple blazed with gold and jewels, and his long fair hair, falling upon his shoulders, was surmounted with a diadem of pearls. But in spite of his magnificence, and the almost unlimited power he now enjoyed as absolute master of that vast empire, he came in with almost the humility of a little child, and walking to the chair of state, remained standing before it until the bishops had all taken their seats again. He must have been very deeply touched, too, as he looked round and saw so many martyr-confessors in the assembly, and yet he knew that faithful and earnest as they might be they were still fallible men, and by no means perfect, or the numbers of letters he had received from them would never have been written. He now drew them from under his mantle, and laid them on the desk before him—a large pile of parchment rolls—and then sent one of the guards for a brazier.

When it was brought he laid them upon the burning coals, and while they were being consumed he turned to the assembly and opening wide his robe he said, "My friends, if I saw one of you committing a fault I would cover him with my mantle lest the others should see it likewise, for it behooveth us not to cause scandals and dissensions by our quarrels. I have burned these letters, and I would that the causes of them were buried, that your deliberations here may be for the peace

DIADEM: *crown*
FALLIBLE MEN: *men who could make errors*
BRAZIER: *a metal pan filled with hot coals*

of the empire and the ruling faithfully Christ's holy Church."

He then delivered a long address in Latin, which was translated into Greek, as many of those present did not understand Latin, and then the council was declared to be open, and each was invited to express his views. The Bishop of Alexandria was one of the first to speak, which, of course, brought a retort from Arius, and he might have borne down every argument of the feeble old man but for his little insignificant-looking deacon, Athanasius. He had not been noticed until he spoke; but no one was likely to forget him again. Arius was foiled at every point by his trenchant little adversary; and the young deacon made more friends and more enemies in one day than it often falls to a man's lot to make in a lifetime.

The Council was continued from day to day, for neither side was willing to give up its opinion, and even the presence of the emperor hardly kept the indignation within bounds when the Thalia of Arius was produced and some of its songs read. Some put their fingers into their ears and closed their eyes in horror; while one good man went so far as to step up to Arius and box his ears, while there was a universal cry for his excommunication.

He was banished from the council at once; and then, when some degree of quietness had been restored, a creed as the exponent of the belief of the

TRENCHANT: *forceful*
EXCOMMUNICATION: *banishment from the Church*
CREED: *a formal statement of beliefs*
EXPONENT: *explanation*

Church was submitted to the Council, and after a good deal of discussion and various modifications, the following creed was adopted as the rule of faith:

"We believe in one God the Father Almighty, Maker of all things visible and invisible; and in one Lord Jesus Christ, the Son of God, begotten of the Father, Only-begotten, that is of the substance of the Father; God of God; Light of Light; Life of Life; very God of very God; begotten, not made; of the same substance with the Father; by whom all things were made, both things in heaven and things in earth; who for us men and our salvation descended and became flesh, and was made man, suffered, and rose again the third day. He ascended into heaven; he cometh to judge the quick and dead. And in the Holy Ghost. But those that say there was a time when he was not; or that he was not before he was begotten; or that he was made from that which hath no being; or who affirm the Son of God to be of any other substance or essence, or created, or variable, or mutable, such persons doth the Catholic and Apostolic Church anathematize."

"I am disappointed!" was the first exclamation of Quadratus to his friend, the giant bishop from the North.

He looked his surprise. "Disappointed!" he repeated in his own Teutonic language.

MUTABLE: *able to change*
ANATHEMATIZE: *curse*

"Yes, I am disappointed in that the Church hath undertaken the task of cursing any man. She will turn persecutor next, and forget her high mission of teaching all men the love of God and the grace of Christ our Saviour."

"It is a high mission, truly," said the Goth; "and if I could only know that my countrymen would receive the message I could die content. I have little need of creeds or anathemas yet," he added, "for I can only teach the first lessons of faith in God; but by and by, perhaps—"

"Nay, nay," interrupted Quadratus; "the world will never be the better for these anathemas. The work of the Church is to bless; we soldiers can curse and fight. Is the Council now closed?" he asked, for he was anxious to have some conversation with Athanasius before his return, and he had been so actively engaged hitherto, that anything beyond the disputed question of Arianism was out of the question at present.

"Nay, the Council meets again tomorrow to discuss the question of whether it is meet and right for a bishop to take a wife, or whether marriage is not unlawful in such as give themselves to the preaching of the Gospel."

"What! would they have the whole world a huge monastery then? Truly these holy fathers have a zeal without knowledge; and if they take not good heed the Church will be injured rather than strengthened by such Councils."

ANATHEMAS: *curses*
MEET: *appropriate*

"Nay, nay, but thou knowest it has not become law yet; some will doubtless oppose this measure, although the hermit-bishops will doubtless favor it."

In this, however, the Gothic bishop was mistaken, for as soon as it was proposed the hermit-bishop, Paphnutius, rose from his seat and limped to the middle of the hall. Turning his disfigured face toward the emperor, and looking round upon the assembly, he exclaimed, "Lay not this heavy burden upon the clergy. 'Marriage is honorable in all,'[1] as Paul himself declares;" and the words thus spoken, by such a man, were sufficient to set the matter aside for that time, at least.

This question being settled, and the creed signed and delivered to the emperor, the Council broke up, and its members began to prepare for their homeward journey. Some were anxious to stay at Rome on the way, for the bishop, Sylvester, had been too ill to attend the Council, being represented there by two presbyters. This had likewise been the case with Alexander of Byzantium, so that neither of the rival cities had taken a very active part in this Council.

The Bishop of Alexandria, with his archdeacon, and their small retinue of slaves, were anxious to cross the sea before the autumn storms rendered the passage dangerous, and so Quadratus obtained leave to accompany them on their journey to the now half-ruinous Byzantium, where they

[1] HEBREWS 13:4

RETINUE: *group of attendants*

would embark in one of the corn ships returning to Alexandria.

At the first opportunity Quadratus, of course, asked about his sister and her husband. "Thou sayest Placidia hath not been heard of yet," he said; "dost thou know whether Lucullus hath made any further inquiries lately?"

"He sent to his agents at Rome and here in Byzantium; for if, as thou fearest, the Jews had carried her off, they would take her to a slave-market as far distant from her home as possible, lest she should be recovered."

"Then thou dost think that all hope of finding her is at an end now," said Quadratus, looking into the young deacon's face as though he would read his answer in his features.

Athanasius shook his head. "I begin to think Melissa is right," he said; "if she were living we should have heard of her I am sure."

"If I could feel sure she was with my mother in heaven my mind would be at rest," said Quadratus with a sigh; "but it is the uncertainty—the suspense—the possibility that she may be suffering in mind and body, that causes me so much anxiety."

Athanasius could not reply, for the mule on which he was riding being suddenly seized with a fit of obstinacy refused to move an inch further; and Quadratus, who preferred walking at all times when it was possible, was about to apply the persuasive force of a good stout stick which he carried, when a train of bullock wagons appeared a short distance behind them, and the drivers began bawling lustily for them to clear the road.

The slaves, who did not understand much of what was said, stood looking helplessly at the bishop and deacon; but Quadratus, who saw that the road must be cleared for the wagons to pass, ordered them to lead the bishop's mule on until they could find a nook in the narrow road where they could wait. Athanasius then got down, and tried his skill at leading his own beast, but neither blows nor coaxing would induce him to move, and then the party stood in the middle of the road, the slaves and the bishop only a little in advance, when the drivers of the wagons came up to them.

"Why dost thou not move the beast out of the way? Knowest thou not we are at work for the emperor?" shouted one.

"Constantine's business can't stand still for a lazy—" but there the man paused, and gazed at Athanasius with a look of awe.

"My friends, we too have been busy about the concerns of the emperor," said Quadratus, anxious to avoid a dispute with these men; "we are now on our way to Byzantium, having been to the Council at Nicæa."

But at the word council the men dropped their ox-goads and fell on their knees before them. "Ye are two of the great bishops whom the emperor

TRAIN: *procession*
BULLOCK WAGONS: *ox-carts*
OX-GOADS: *long rods with pointed ends used to prod oxen*

hath commanded all men to help forward, and whom this great God of the Christians hath given power to work miracles greater than those performed by Jupiter himself," and they reverently kissed the hem of Athanasius' garment as they spoke.

"Nay, I am no bishop," said Quadratus with a smile; "and as for the miracles that have been performed, who told thee of them?"

"Those who witnessed them," said one of the wagoners. "But we pray thee hinder us not, for we are bearing great treasures of marble and porphyry to build the new Byzantium, for the emperor is in great haste to have it rebuilt."

"We will not hinder thee longer than to move this obstinate mule out of the road," said Quadratus; "and if thou wilt lend us thine aid doubtless he may soon be brought to a more tractable state."

But instead of taking hold of the mule the men drew further back, slowly shaking their heads. They were not willing to hold the head of even a beast ridden by a bishop. True, they had been baptized, and went to church as often as they could. They had received their white baptismal robe and twenty gold pieces as a gift from the emperor, but they would not draw too near a bishop, who might turn them into mules where they stood as easily as they could restore one to life, and this one of them had done on his way to this same Council, they had been solemnly assured. In vain Quadratus

TRACTABLE: *yielding*

protested that they were in possession of no such supernatural power, and that neither of them was a bishop, he having gone on before. Still the men held back.

"Dost thou think if we possessed the power thou sayest we should stand here so long trying to make this beast move by means of a stick in the same way that ye would?" asked the young soldier, beginning to lose his patience.

The men shook their heads but still looked unconvinced.

At last Quadratus took refuge in the orders issued by the emperor, and which had been publicly proclaimed in every town through which the travelers were likely to pass. "If thou dost not help us forward in this difficulty thou wilt be guilty of breaking the law of the empire," he said; "and I will tell ye now that I am one of the emperor's guard."

Consternation, fear, and awe, mingled with a desire to obey their emperor's command, was plainly visible in the face of each; but they drew near the mule, and a few touches from their experienced hands were quite enough to set the obstinate brute in motion; but Athanasius had walked on to join the bishop, for the poor old man was easily alarmed at anything of this kind, and so Quadratus led the mule himself, and the wagons came slowly afterward.

He could not refrain from laughing when he

related all that had passed to Athanasius, for although he had witnessed most of the affair he could not understand much of what the wagoner had said.

"Who could have spread such a tale as this concerning our power of performing miracles!" exclaimed the bishop.

"It is mere idle gossip," said Athanasius; "these men have heard something they know not what, and have made up this story about the mule being raised to life."

"Their reverence for the clergy is real enough— too real, I think," observed the soldier seriously.

"Too real!" repeated Athanasius.

"Yes, it is only equaled by their ignorance, which is the sole excuse for it. God is only in their minds evidently another name for Jupiter, and I suppose they may be taken as a fair sample of those to whom our emperor presents a white robe and twenty gold pieces as a baptismal gift. Twenty thousand men, besides women and children, received this gift last year. But dost thou think these are such Christians as gathered in the caves of the desert or an empty fruit-boat on the Nile during the times of Diocletian?"

"And wouldst thou have those times over again?" asked Athanasius.

"God forbid! but this I would say, the Church is not so prosperous that we can afford to quarrel over logical disquisitions; and the broad mark of separation that is arising between the clergy and their flocks is to be regretted. It was not so in the old days. Then the minister was the servant of all, and the brother of all; but now he is looked at with superstitious awe by the ignorant, and makes himself a lord over God's heritage."

"There is truth in what thou dost say, Quadratus," assented the young deacon; and the whole party fell into a thoughtful silence.

Chapter VIII

The Prefect of Carthage

THE noonday sun was pouring down its fierce rays upon the streets of Carthage, an important city still although an appanage of Rome, and scarcely less splendid than when she sent forth her brave sons under Hannibal to dispute the sovereignty of the world with her (now) Roman mistress. Nearly five hundred years had passed since she stooped her proud neck beneath the yoke; but in art, and learning, and commerce, she was almost as flourishing under a Roman prefect as under her former rulers.

The grain of mustard seed, from which sprang the tree whose branches now spread over the empire, had early found a lodgment in Carthage, and persecutions had prevailed there as well as everywhere else. But under Constantine no prefect who was known to have been a persecutor could hope to retain his post, and most of these officers found it conducive to their temporal advancement to become Christians, in name at least,

LODGMENT: *foothold*

and to secure the favor and patronage of the bishops at all costs.

Victor, the prefect of Carthage, was one who professed a great love for the new national faith, and a reverence for the bishop, Cecilius, that nothing could equal, and certainly he had shown him every possible attention, and himself accompanied him to the place of embarkation when he left the city to attend the Council. He was now returning from this short journey, tired, hot, and dusty, cursing himself for his folly in going.

"Carthage is free now to disport herself as she pleaseth for a few weeks or months at least, and we will let the old gods see that they are not quite forgotten, and the people shall know what life is once more," Victor said to his friend as they entered the palace and called for wine and the dice-board.

"Thou dost forget the monks and deacons, and all the motley crew of the parabolani the old man hath left behind."

"I care not for them now that I am free of Cecilius. It is not often I can do as I like, and I mean not to miss the present opportunity. I have a tiger in the *vivarium*, and we will have him out with a few of the old gladiators if they have not quite forgotten the use of the sword. Then we will have one of the old plays in the theater, 'Venus Rising from the Sea,' or something of the same kind, just to remind the people of what used to be before monks and bishops ruled the world."

DISPORT: *amuse*
MOTLEY: *greatly varied*
VIVARIUM: *an indoor enclosure for viewing animals*

His companion rubbed his hands delightedly. "Thou art a bold fellow, Victor," he said, "but be careful not to go too far."

"Trust my sagacity for that. Thou seest the present time affords me such an excellent opportunity and excuse too. The emperor celebrates the twentieth year of his reign next month; what more natural than that they should insist upon going to the basilica and worship before the Augustenium, where the Cæsars are enshrined. From the Augustenium to the amphitheater is but a short step, and the rest will follow as a matter of course, I yielding reluctantly to the popular demand in order to prevent a tumult."

"Victor, thou oughtest to be emperor of Africa instead of prefect of Carthage," said his friend admiringly; "it is all so very cleverly conceived and arranged. But surely, if thou dost take so much trouble to please the people, thou art going to allow thyself a little liberty in the matter of pleasures," he added.

"To be sure I am, and thou canst make it known, my friend, among all thy acquaintance, that the prefect is blind to any breach of the strict rules laid down by Cecilius concerning the conduct of their entertainments. By the way, I heard that an old Jewess came into the city last night with a fresh lot of girls—quite choice samples in their way—picked up in all the fashionable slave-markets of the empire."

SAGACITY: *wisdom*

"She will ask an extravagant price for them; these Jews always do."

"They are hard at driving a bargain; but I shall send for her, and look at her slaves without telling her I am wishing to purchase any."

"As if she would not be cunning enough to find it out for herself and charge thee accordingly."

"Very well, then, I must squeeze it out of the people—put a tax upon fresh melons or some trifle, for I mean to have two or three more slaves, and enjoy myself while I can;" and as he spoke he languidly adjusted his flower crown, and threw the dice upon the board.

"I wonder what the old woman would ask for a fine girl of seventeen, who had never been into the markets," he said presently.

"If she had one, thou meanest."

"O! she is sure to have one—at least I will ask her."

"Better send at once, then, or somebody else may get her," suggested his friend, who saw he was likely to lose the stakes if the game was continued.

"I think I will," lazily responded the prefect; and sending a slave for parchment and a papyrus reed, he soon wrote a letter, commanding the Jewess to bring some of her human chattels to his palace the next morning for his inspection. This was sent by another slave, who was directed to inquire of the guard who had command of the Jewish quarter

LANGUIDLY: *lazily*
CHATTELS: *property*

where the old woman had gone to lodge.

There was little difficulty in finding old Deborah; and the slave presented the letter and received her assurances that she would be at his excellency's palace early in the morning to receive his commands in person, and then the withered old hag hobbled into a side passage, and taking a key from her girdle unlocked the door of a large room where some twenty girls of all ages and all countries were sitting, lying, or walking about. There was a fair-haired girl from the far-off barbarous Britain, learning a lesson in Greek from a proud, haughty-looking Alexandrian.

"Placidia thou wilt not leave me," she whispered. "Thou hast taught me about thy God, but I shall forget Him, and think only of our forest spirits and the Druids if thou dost go away."

"God will take care of thee, my Imogene," said her companion as the old woman drew near to where they were sitting.

"Come, now, girls, see if ye cannot play a merry tune, and have a dance to amuse old Deborah; for there is little enough going on in the streets since these accursed Nazarenes got the upper hand in the world," and she darted an angry look at the two, who drew closer into the corner at her approach.

The room was furnished with divans on either side, and the old woman seated herself on one of these, while one of the girls fetched a double flute

NAZARENES: *Christians*
DIVANS: *backless couches*

from a pedestal standing near, and soon commenced a soft, dreamy tune, while her companions commenced a slow-measured dance, delicate
tinklings of the silver bells on their wrists and an-
kles keeping time with the flute.

"There, now, a little quicker," said the old woman. "We shall have a merry time yet, my girls, for
the old Nazarene bishop hath gone to this gathering of monks," and again she darted a look of
triumph toward the two in the corner.

As the dancing grew quicker and more lively
the old woman signified her approval by clapping
her hands, and then some wine was fetched and
handed round to all but the two in the corner, who
seemed thankful to be thus ignored. By degrees
the dancers drew farther away from them, until at
last Imogene ventured to speak once more.

"Placidia, thou wilt not let them take me from
thee," she said.

"I will take care of thee as long as I can; but
didst thou not hear, the bishop hath gone away to
that—that—O! my Imogene, my last hope of rescue
hath failed," and it was with difficulty the poor
girl restrained her sobs.

"Hush, hush, old Deborah will hear thee," whispered her companion, "and it cannot be thy last
hope, for God is here in Carthage, and He will
take care of us, will He not?"

Imogene asked the question very anxiously, and
seemed at a loss to understand her companion's

distress, for Placidia had taught her that the great God was always near to help His children in every time of trouble, and she had believed it most implicitly. For Placidia, therefore, to be so cast down because the Bishop of Carthage was absent, was a puzzle to the simple young Briton, but, at length, she said, "Is it, my Placidia, that God hath gone away with the bishop that thou art in such sorrow?"

"No, God is here still," answered Placidia.

"Then we are safe; we must be, thou knowest, for He is our 'refuge and strength,'[1] and He will deliver us and take care of us." Imogene put her arms around Placidia's neck, and whispered to her the words she had learned from her lips, and in that hour of darkness she experienced the truth of that promise, "He that watereth shall be watered also himself,"[2] for Imogene helped her to rest upon the help and protection of God once more, so that when she repeated her question, "Will not God take care of us?" she was able to say with confidence, "Yes, dear child, He will. He is ever faithful to His promises. But I am faithless, Imogene—as faithless now as I was proud before."

"Wert thou proud? Wert thou a lady in Alexandria?" asked the girl.

"Yes, but it was not of that I was proud, but of being the daughter of a martyr and the sister of a hermit, and I resolved to become a nun, and leave the world to live in the desert, that men might talk

[1] PSALM 46:1   [2] PROVERBS 11:25

of my holiness as they often talked of theirs."

"And thou didst go to the desert," said Imogene.

"Nay, but my mother wished me to stay with her and so I submitted, but not very willingly, and shut myself up in the tower alone. When my brother, who is one of the emperor's guards, came to visit us I refused to see him at first, for I thought he was of the world I had renounced; and when, at the request of my mother, I did consent to see him, I treated him so coldly, that poor Quadratus was sorely grieved about it, I know. After that interview, at which he parted with me in much anger, I only saw him once, and that was on the dreadful day of the riot. He fetched me down to the inner court, where my mother was lying, and bade me watch beside her while he guarded the door with the slaves; but he had scarcely left us before my mother opened her eyes for a moment and looked at me, and the next minute death had closed them forever. Then there was a noise of fighting that I scarcely observed until one of the slaves ran in and told me that Quadratus had been killed, and before I could move a party of Jews followed him, and I was hurried away, quite unconscious of where I was taken."

"And thou hast never been to Alexandria since?" asked Imogene in a low voice.

"Nay, it was not likely they would take me to where my friends would be sure to find me. These

Jews are too clever, and play into each other's hands too much to allow their victims any chance of escape. I have been passed from one to another and taken from place to place, so that it would be impossible for any trace to be discovered even if my sister should try," added Placidia with a sigh.

This hope, which at first had been indulged, was fast dying away now, and her only chance of escape was in appealing to the bishop of one of the cities; and she had hoped this visit to Carthage would afford her the opportunity she so anxiously longed for.

The next morning they were awakened early to dress themselves with all care, to be in readiness for the prefect. Placidia and Imogene were obliged to put on the white linen tunics and silver ornaments like the rest, and neither of them could help looking very pretty as they stood side by side, presenting such a striking contrast as they did. Imogene, with her delicate, fair skin, and her bright, golden hair, and Placidia, with her wealth of raven curls and dark flashing eyes—almost defiant they had grown lately—for, slave though she was, neither of her owners had been able to bend her to their will, and Deborah, even now, was secretly uneasy about the issue of this transaction.

"She will be worth all the trouble, certainly, if I can sell her to this prefect, for she will bring a nice round sum in gold pieces, she is such a splendid girl," muttered the old woman as she adjusted her

RAVEN: *shiny black*

turban preparatory to going out.

She was going to the palace by herself first, for she was anxious to know her customer before introducing her merchandise, for she had other things to sell besides slaves. Rare old wines of the true Falernian flavor; choice gems, that would grace an emperor's diadem; silk stuffs and shawls, that were fit to wrap the daintiest lady; and poisoned daggers, that would speedily end the life of any inconvenient friend or foe—all these old Deborah had brought with her to Carthage, hoping to drive a good bargain, but she was not going to let the prefect know all this at once.

Victor, on his part, thought himself quite equal in cunning to any old Jewess in the world; and, as soon as she had been ushered into his presence, asked what she had brought with her to the city.

"A few slaves, your excellency; a very few, for I am a poor old woman, as thou mayest see," whined Deborah, displaying her ragged old damask robe rather ostentatiously.

"The Jews always are poor, according to their own account, and yet ye contrive to make us Christians your debtors pretty often," said the prefect. "But now about these slaves—hast thou any worth looking at?"

"I have two or three from Armenia that would suit your excellency," said the old woman humbly.

"I am tired of Armenians. Hast thou any others?"

FALERNIAN: *wine made from grapes grown on the slopes of Mount Falernus in Italy*
OSTENTATIOUSLY: *showily*

"There are just two from Italy—true Roman maidens they are."

"Worse and worse," said the prefect, "what's the next?"

The old woman shook her head. "I could not recommend the next," she said, "she hath given me so much trouble with her airs about being a lady, and an Alexandrian—of course it is all false—though she does come of a rare old stock, and a haughty one, too, as any may see who are skilled in such matters."

"Untamed, is she—never been into the market before?" inquired Victor.

"I should like to see the man, Jew or Gentile, who could make Placidia stand up in any market. No, no, Placidia would not suit thee I am sure. There is a little Briton, too, but she is nearly as bad, so that I am afraid—"

"Go and fetch the young Briton and this Placidia at once," interrupted the prefect imperiously; "it may be they will suit me after all."

The old woman went out shaking her head, but internally chuckling over the success of her ruse. "He hath fallen into the trap," she said half-aloud, "and I shall get rid of this Placidia now."

IMPERIOUSLY: *commandingly*
RUSE: *trick*

Chapter IX

Something New

A SLAVE! Placidia looked more like an insult-ed empress as she stood before Victor a few hours later, for the old woman had succeeded in making a good bargain with him and getting rid of her troublesome property. She and Imogene had both been disposed of, and the prefect was already beginning to repent of his bargain, for Placidia was by no means so manageable as he thought he could make her.

"She looks like a goddess herself," he exclaimed, when telling some of his friends of his first inter-view with his new slave. "She dared me to approach her, and threatened to inform the bishop and call down all the thunders of the Church if I ventured too near one who was a holy nun."

"A nun, is she!" exclaimed one, with a prolonged whistle. "No wonder the old woman left Carthage as soon as the bargain was completed."

"Why, the Church could not interfere, and—"

"I would advise thee not to come to an issue

PLACIDIA BEFORE THE PREFECT OF CARTHAGE

with the Church or the bishop either, for there is no knowing what they may be able to do;" interrupted one of his friends warningly.

"It is a hard case, I think, that a man cannot do as he likes with his own slave," grumbled the prefect.

"But if she is a nun—a spouse of Christ, as these fanatics would call her—they would question thy right to hold her as a slave."

"Nay, but I have the papers, the receipt from the old Jewess," said Victor.

"Ah, but how did this old woman become possessed of her? Bought her in the regular way of trade, thou wilt say; and the tale might do for thee, but it would not do for Cecilian. He would hear the girl's story—where she took the vows, and send to some other bishop to have it confirmed or disproved, and then if it should be the former, and thou hadst laid a finger on the girl, where wouldst thou be with the power these Christians have over the emperor's mind?"

Victor looked rueful. "I wish I had never seen the girl," he said uneasily. "There is the little Briton, too—a heap of money those two have cost me."

"The old woman made a good thing of it, I have no doubt," remarked his friend.

"She did not want me to have those two," said Victor.

"Thou wouldst say she pretended to be unwilling, cried them up with one breath and down with the next on purpose to edge thee on. I know these Jews, I have had dealings with them, my Victor, and hate them as cordially as they hate us."

"The old woman was civil enough. I don't see why they should hate us," said the prefect sulkily. He was ready to dispute any statement just now if only for the sake of venting his ill humor.

"O, she was civil enough, I dare say. I never had anything to complain of on the score of civility; but they hate us nonetheless, and glory in the idea that we are all doomed to eternal punishment. Of course she would not care whether the girl was a nun or a goddess; Christian and pagan are alike to her, so that she makes a good bargain; but I warn thee, Victor, to be careful, for none knows the power of the Church now, and, of course, we are all Christians too," he added, with a short laugh.

The prefect, however, was in no laughing mood. "The obstinacy of this girl will upset all my plans, for I meant her to be Venus rising from the sea, and the little Briton would make a splendid sea nymph too; but now—"

"Better disappoint the people and put up with their grumbling than lose thy prefecture, and it might come to that if she is a nun."

"I wish there were no nuns; a man doesn't know now whether—"

"Whether he can insult a woman with impunity," said his companion with a covert sneer.

But Victor did not notice this. "There never was

IMPUNITY: *no fear of punishment*
COVERT: *hidden*

such a fuss made about purity, and honor, and virtue in the old days; a man could do as he liked
then, but now—"

"The Church hath stepped in—this new power
in the State—with new laws and new ideas, and
one of the greatest of these is that a woman is no
longer to be a man's toy and slave, but sacred as
the vestals of Rome if they place themselves under
the protection of the Church."

"Yes, that is just what they have done," assented
Victor; "and I say it is undue interference with a
man's rights."

"But we shall have to put up with it, nevertheless. Now tell me what arrangements thou hast
made with the gladiators, and forget the girl."

Victor gave him a detailed account of the interview he had had with the old master of the school,
and what he had promised on behalf of his pupils.
"There will be a fight with the cestus, and another
with the net and trident. I wish I had a couple of
criminals for that tiger," he suddenly added.

"Criminals seem to be growing scarce, like every other luxury in these degenerate days."

"They never are to be had when they are wanted,"
grumbled the prefect. "These monks go prowling
about the streets among the poor and sick, feeding and nursing them, and then exhorting them
to be patient and honest, so that our prisons are
well-nigh empty at the present time."

"And to get up a false charge against anybody

VESTALS: *priestesses of Vesta, the Roman goddess of homes*
CESTUS: *a leather glove weighted with iron or lead*
TRIDENT: *three-pronged spear*

for the sake of a good spectacle would be to bring a whole hornet's nest of monks and bishops about our ears."

"Constantine himself would doubtless be informed of the paltry affair by these meddlers. We shall have to give up the criminal I am afraid," sighed Victor, "and be content with the tiger being dispatched by the gladiators. It will be a tame affair, I fear," he added, with another sigh of disgust.

Meanwhile Placidia had been encouraging her companion to trust in the Lord for deliverance, although her own heart well-nigh failed her now, as she thought of the hopelessness of her captivity and the power of the man into whose hands she had fallen. She had heard of the cruelty and oppression practiced by these Roman governors in their irresponsible power, that almost made her hair stand on end with horror as she recalled them; but she did not tell Imogene any of these stories, for the poor girl was already alarmed enough.

If Placidia could only have known the effect her declaration of being a nun had had upon her master she would have been more hopeful, but she was as yet unaware of this new law—this new protection that the Church had thrown around women— partial and slight in its effects it might be, when we consider the magnitude of the evil; but still it was a great step in advance, the first step toward the raising of women to a higher level, although, perhaps, few perceived it in those days.

PALTRY: *insignificant*

"We have only God to look to for help and deliverance now," said Placidia, "so let us pray to Him, my Imogene, for He can deliver us from this palace as He did His servant Peter from prison;" and as she spoke she raised her eyes and hands and prayed aloud, while Imogene mutely but tearfully joined in her supplication.

When she had concluded she sat down and drew Imogene's head upon her shoulder. "Will God be sure to hear, Placidia?" whispered the girl as she looked toward the door, expecting, perhaps, to see some angel visitant entering even then.

"Yes, God is sure to hear," answered Placidia, but the next moment a troubled look came into her face.

The watchful eyes of her companion saw it. "What is it—what is the matter?" she asked.

"I was thinking of thy question, Imogene, and of what I used to hear in the Church of Alexandria. It is more than a year since I was in a church," she added; "but I remember so well our deacon, Athanasius, how careful he was to make us remember the greatness and glory of the Lord Jesus Christ."

"Wert thou likely to forget it, then?" asked Imogene.

Placidia would not tell her young convert of the dispute about Arianism, but merely answered, "Perhaps we were, only I think we began to go to the other extreme, and forget his loving-kindness and tender mercy. I was thinking of Athanasius and his sermons while thou wert speaking, and

VISITANT: *visitor*

wondered whether I had not been wrong lately in thinking so much of the love of Christ. I know not how it was," went on Placidia, talking to herself rather than to Imogene, "but after my mother died and I was all alone—a slave among the Jews—the power of Christ did not comfort me so much. I seemed to want a mother's love, and I am afraid I have been thinking the Lord Christ had this mother-love for me."

"Thou tellest me the Lord Christ did love us like that!" exclaimed Imogene sharply. "Thou saidst there were words written like these: 'When my father and my mother forsake me, then the Lord will take me up!'[1] Thou saidst that meant He would be mother and father too, and how could He be a mother if He did not love us like one?"

"Forgive me, Imogene, for making thee doubt the love of God our Saviour," said Placidia tenderly, seeing the look of distress in the sweet, pale face of her friend. "I will think more of this love again, and if—if I am wrong—"

"Mayest thou be wrong after all?" asked Imogene anxiously.

"No, dear; Christ loves us, and died for us—died that we might live. It was not that I doubted His love, but whether we might go to Him with every little care and trouble, whether if He were so great and glorious He could—" and there she stopped.

"What wouldst thou say, my Placidia?" asked Imogene anxiously; "is thy God like our forest

[1] PSALM 27:10

spirits—too great and powerful to be troubled with the sorrows of poor slaves?"

"No, no! Hush, Imogene, our Lord Christ died the death of a slave, and so He can feel for us in all our sorrows."

"Then what dost thou mean?" asked Imogene, still very much puzzled. "Is it that we may not pray to Him so often?"

But Placidia again shook her head. She could not define the filmy doubt that so often obscured her spiritual vision, and so she wisely gave up the attempt, seeing that it would only unsettle the faith of Imogene and render her unhappy. She had told her the story of the Lord's life on earth; of His love to little children; of His compassion for the hungry and weary multitude; of His tenderness with Martha and Mary at the grave of their brother; and while teaching her these lessons of His love and sympathy she had forgotten for a time the great distance that seemed to intervene between them now, and her heart had laid down its burden of sorrow and care and anxiety at His feet, and she had basked in the sunshine of that love she had tried to reveal to Imogene.

As for the young Briton, she received it all with the earnest simplicity of a little child. Her articles of faith were very few. Christ loved her and died to save her, and she loved Him, and so to hear Placidia speak now as though there was a doubt of this troubled her exceedingly.

She had never heard of Arius and his abstruse doctrine that had set Athanasius on fire to defend the assailed honor of his Lord and Master, and, therefore, she was the more troubled as she failed to understand the reason of this sudden doubt in Placidia. Their talk over this matter—for Placidia was determined to set Imogene's mind at rest—was interrupted an hour or two later by the entrance of a slave, who commanded them to follow him to the presence of his master.

Victor looked flushed and angry, and took a draught of wine from a jeweled cup as they entered hand in hand. "Ye make a pretty contrast and might have an easy time of it with me if ye liked," he said, eyeing them from head to foot as they stood before him.

Placidia did not reply, but her eyes flashed and her cheeks grew crimson. "Thou wouldst make a splendid Hebe," said Victor in a tone of admiration. "Come, now, be reasonable. Thou wert not in earnest when thou saidst thou wert a nun."

Placidia saw that this declaration had been of some use at least, and she determined to press her advantage. "Not in earnest!" she repeated; "dost thou suppose I have no more conscience than thou, or that I—"

"Come, come; forget not thou art my slave," interrupted Victor.

"I am a nun of the Church of Alexandria. Send for Cecilian, thy bishop, and let him duly inquire

HEBE: *the Greek goddess of youth*

of that whereof I affirm. I demand this at thy hands as a Christian ruler and magistrate. I have never before been able to state how I was stolen from Alexandria in a riot by a party of Jews, but I state this now to thee, the prefect of Carthage, and in the name of the Church and the emperor I demand justice."

"Justice!" repeated Victor, staring at the two girls in blank amazement. He might have laughed at her demand, and ordered her to be whipped for her temerity in speaking to him thus—might even have reached for the strip of rhinoceros hide that he always kept at hand and inflicted some chastisement upon her himself but for the hints of his friends about the power of the Church and the danger of touching a nun. "Justice!" he repeated again after a pause; "thou dost talk about justice. I wonder who will repay me the gold pieces thou hast cost me."

"My friends will pay any reasonable sum to ransom me," said Placidia; but the words were not spoken very confidently, for she suddenly thought of the reproaches she had heaped upon her sister for marrying Lucullus, and with what scorn and contempt she had met all the advances of her brother-in-law, and that these were now her only relatives.

The hesitation of her manner made Victor decide in his own mind not to trust to this hope of a ransom for regaining his money, but at the same

TEMERITY: *boldness*

time he resolved to get rid of his troublesome bargain without delay, for he could see that Placidia
might be the cause of trouble between himself and
the bishop if she remained at Carthage very long.

To Victor's great relief a party of Jews on their
way to Syria reached the city a few days afterward,
and from these he was glad to get a third of the
price he had paid old Deborah for his two slaves,
and so they once more found themselves in the
hands of a new owner.

To Placidia it was no surprise to find they again
reverted to the old Jewess, and were to be taken by
her to Syria; for she knew that the woman had numerous agents traveling about, and Placidia was
too thankful to escape from the palace of Victor
to care very much where she was next taken.

Chapter X

The Parting

DEBORAH, the Jewess, whose one aim in life was to make money, chuckled loudly over her cleverness when Placidia and Imogene again passed into her hands; and she thought if she could overreach a few more people, as she had the prefect of Carthage, Placidia might yet prove a profitable investment in spite of her obstinacy. The old woman did not treat her slaves unkindly, except that their confinement was rather close, and they never had a chance to escape from her power. But for this and the constant change of travel Placidia would have sunk under her affliction; but by degrees she was growing more reconciled to her fate, and when at last, after a lengthened stay at Cypress, they reached Cæsarea, and she heard that they were going to the spot sacred to every Christian—Jerusalem—her heart swelled with joy and thankfulness, for pilgrimages to the sacred hill of Calvary were already becoming fashionable, and the wish to go to the Holy Land had

OVERREACH: *get the better of by trickery*
CLOSE: *strict*

been almost as strong as her desire to retire to the desert.

This land of Palestine was holy to Deborah as well as to Placidia. It was the land of promise—the land of David and Solomon; and though trodden down by the Gentiles now, the time would come when the Jews would again be restored to its ancient hills and valleys. It was this hope that led so many of her countrymen to plot, and scheme, and lie, and cheat; for wealth was power, and the power they longed for was to free their land from Gentile dominion, and to see the ancient line of their kings once more seated on the throne of David.

Old Deborah longed as ardently as any of her race for the consummation of this hope. For this she toiled and labored—lent countless hoards of wealth to luxurious Roman governors, who she hoped by and by would lend their aid to the plans now sleeping in many a busy brain. It was touching to see the change in the world-hardened, callous old woman when she stepped ashore and once more breathed the air of her native land. The lines of her face relaxed, and there was the dew of tears in her dim old eyes as she stooped and kissed the sacred earth. It was a beautiful land, still beautiful in spite of its desolation; and when at length their journey was over and they reached the top of a gentle slope that commanded a view of the ruins in the valley beyond—all that remained of "the city of the Great King"[1]—Placidia could not wholly

---

[1] MATTHEW 5:35
ARDENTLY: *passionately*
CONSUMMATION: *fulfillment*

restrain her tears, while old Deborah wept aloud.

It soon transpired, however, that it was not merely to weep over the ruins of the sacred city that the old Jewess had journeyed all these miles. In the little half-desolate village that had sprung up near the site of the ancient city a large company of pilgrims had now gathered, for the empress-mother, Helena, in spite of her seventy-nine years, had come on a pilgrimage with a large retinue of slaves and guards, and with some of these, or with Helena herself, the Jewess thought she might probably drive a good bargain.

Her tents were pitched near the little village of huts and flat-roofed houses, but before they had settled themselves they were surprised to see a long procession slowly winding its way down from the direction of Calvary, and as they drew nearer Placidia could see that many of them were monks and Roman guards, and that near the front walked a white-haired, majestic-looking old lady, whose purple-bordered dress indicated her relation to the imperial family. Could this be Helena, the mother of Constantine?

The question was soon answered by some of the villagers telling the old Jewess that the Nazarenes had been excavating the top of Mount Calvary, and were now bringing down a cross that had been found there.

"A cross!" repeated Placidia; "can it be the very cross on which the Lord was crucified?"

But Deborah turned upon her a look of disgust. "The Nazarenes will believe anything after that," she said, "as though it would have lain there three hundred years and now be found perfect;" and with a muttered curse as she watched the procession wind its slow length along she turned into the tent and ordered Placidia and Imogene to follow, for if this company of Christians were so near she would not trust them out of her sight until they were disposed of. She hoped to sell them both to the empress-mother, and for this purpose she went out early the next morning and met some of the attendants on their way to the sacred mount to pray, for no Jews were allowed to enter the presence of the august old lady herself.

Of course she had a very plausible tale to tell as to the way the two Christian captives came into her hands; and she so far touched the sympathies of her auditors that later in the day a command was sent to her to take the little British maiden to the imperial residence.

No mention was made of Placidia, and so she ventured to remind the messenger that she had two Christian slaves. But the cunning and avarice of the Jews were too well-known for them to take much heed of the hint. If Imogene was a Briton and a Christian, doubtless Helena would purchase her, for she had a tender regard for those barbarians, the man said; but she had no need of any others, and she advised the old woman to journey

AUGUST: *majestic*
AUDITORS: *listeners*
AVARICE: *greed*

further on without delay, as the Jews were more than ever hated now since the true cross had been found, and what the Lord had suffered thus presented so palpably before them.

Deborah sniffed and grunted, but asked a large sum for Imogene, whom she professed herself unwilling to take from Placidia. The poor girl herself was very unwilling to leave the friend who had been as a mother, sister, and teacher to her, and she cried bitterly when she thought it might be the last time she would ever look on that sweet, grave face. Placidia, too, was deeply moved, for she had learned to love the little clinging, affectionate girl very dearly; but she knew that such a shelter and refuge might never be found again if this were lost, and so she begged her to stop her tears and look smiling and pleasant, for fear the empress-mother should be displeased at her sadness.

As she had hoped and prayed, Imogene was purchased by Helena to be sent back to her own land and friends, that she might tell them the wonderful news of God's love to man which she had learned from the lips of Placidia.

The poor nun smiled faintly when she heard this. "My life hath not been quite in vain," she said, "and it may be God will take me from this earth to join my mother in heaven very soon."

"Not until we have reached Antioch and I have found a customer for thee, I hope," said old Deborah, with a grim smile, as she overheard these

PALPABLY: *visibly*

words; "thou mayest die then as soon as thou wilt," she added, "for I shall not be the loser."

Whether she thought there was any danger of her slave dying shortly, or whether she deemed it wise to take the hint given her by Helena's attendant, she resolved to travel northward without delay, and if she could not dispose of Placidia by private contract to sell her publicly in the market, for she had grown tired of taking her from place to place.

It was a long and toilsome journey from Judea to Antioch, and, with the exception of a short stay at Damascus they pressed on with all speed, for Deborah was anxious to reach it as soon as possible, and the old woman heaved a sigh of relief when the distant slope of the rocky Mount Silphius slowly rose upon their view.

As they drew nearer, the outline of the far-famed city of Antioch became visible—walls of enormous height and thickness spanning the deep ravines of the mountain; and before the gates were reached, the celebrated groves of Daphne, beyond the walls, that begirt with laurels, cypresses, and myrtles the great shrine dedicated to Apollo and Diana, could be plainly seen.

Old Deborah amused herself by telling Placidia of the grand festivals held in honor of those gods only a few years before, when not only the sacred groves, but the whole city, was crowded with worshipers and revelers, who danced round

DAPHNE: *a nymph in Greek mythology who was turned into a laurel tree*
BEGIRT: *surrounded*

the midsummer fires, and spent money lavishly with the old Jewess, which was, of course, all she cared for, and why she so bitterly lamented the establishment of the Christian faith.

"Not that it will last," went on the old woman spitefully; "such a dull, monotonous religion, with nothing to attract men to it—no music, no festivals, few statues in the churches, no amusements but the dull life of a nun, or hermit, to offer to its followers—how can it live?"

Placidia did not venture to reply, and the old woman went on: "Thou hast no dances in thy worship, no splendor of gold and jewels, no mysteries beyond what the poorest may witness if they have only been baptized; and to whom dost thou give thy highest adoration?—a Nazarene carpenter, who died the death of a slave under an insignificant Roman governor. Is it likely such a religion will last? Constantine may make it serve his own ends, because the old faiths have been slowly dying, and he knew the vulgar herd must worship something; but by and by, when the empire as well as the gods come to an end—and it is dying, girl, dying, decaying of its own rottenness and corruption," almost screamed the old woman. "It is tottering, sinking, falling, like a sick man, and a few more years will see the end. Dost thou hear me, girl?—the end—the end of this empire and this religion, and then—then shall the throne of David be established, and his enemies shall lick the dust. O for a few more years to see this with my eyes before this worn-out old body be laid in the dust! Thou mayest—thou wilt live to see it," she said, turning suddenly upon Placidia, "and when it comes thou wilt know that Deborah was a prophetess."

By this time the gate of the city was reached, and the bustle of entrance broke off the old woman's talk, while Placidia looked up in silent wonder at the columns of rock overhanging the town, and which, by the help of a little Greek art, had been formed into a crowned head, and called the head of Charon.

But even this was soon forgotten as they entered the principal street, and saw the magnificence of its towers and temples, baths and villas, and the evidence of wealth and luxury that met them on every hand. Placidia had been used to the grandeur of Alexandria, but that was fairly eclipsed by this "Queen of the East," this "City of God," for she suddenly remembered that it had also been called by this name, and that a Christian bishop presided over the Church here.

If this latter fact had not been remembered it would soon have been made known to Placidia, for the whole city was astir with the news that was now thrilling every heart in the empire. The true cross had been found by the empress-mother, Helena, and was being conveyed, with other precious relics, to the new capital, Byzantium.

Hymns and anthems were sung in all the

CHARON: *the ferryman in Greek mythology who ferried the dead to Hades, the land of the dead*

churches to celebrate the discovery of this precious treasure, and in Antioch special sermons were preached by the bishop, and *agape*, or lovefeasts, were held in every direction. But no one came to invite poor Placidia to one of these, for on the day of the great celebration she was sent to the slave-market of Antioch to take her place among the groups of domestics, dancing-girls, field laborers, or water-carriers, whichever it was deemed she was most fitted for, the Jewess having decided to sell off all her slaves and rest at Antioch for a time.

Placidia hoped she might be purchased for a domestic servant in a Christian family, and the first of these wishes was gratified but not the second. A citizen of Antioch bought her to take charge of his children, the fact of her being a Christian being taken as a recommendation, although he still adhered to the worship of the old gods himself, and wished his children to do the same.

The news of the cross having been found on Mount Calvary reached Alexandria in due course, but it was with a chastened gladness that the Church rejoiced, for death had laid its hand upon the veteran hermit-bishop, Alexander, and men were looking around for a worthy successor—one who would withstand Arianism and uphold the creed of Nicæa, even against the emperor himself if it were necessary.

DOMESTICS: *household slaves*
CHASTENED: *subdued*

That the choice should fall upon Athanasius surprised no one perhaps but those who thought an advanced age a necessary qualification, and to these the choice of a young deacon, little more than six and twenty, was a great shock in spite of his fitness in all other particulars and the active part he took in the late Council.

Quadratus was on a visit to his native city when Alexander died, and so he went to the cathedral church of Baucalis, where the ceremony of installing the patriarchs of Alexandria always took place. This installation of Athanasius was more grand and imposing than any that had preceded it, for each year added something to the outer ritual of the Church now—something to attract and appeal to the senses of those who had little real love for Christ, but had conformed outwardly to the usages of Christianity, because it was not only the national faith but likewise fashionable, and the only road open to fortune and success. For the sake of these the Church was growing very accommodating, not only in its ritual, but in the adoption of heathen feasts and festivals and calling them by sacred names, a custom in which no danger was then foreseen, but which even Athanasius countenanced at least, for, in his great anxiety to preserve the purity of the Church's doctrines and liberty, he failed to see the evil tendency of practices borrowed from the old heathen worship, that many were still somewhat unwilling to give up.

COUNTENANCED: *tolerated*

It was a solemn, almost a ghastly sight to witness the dead patriarch as he sat enthroned and Athanasius kneeling before him to have the dead hand placed upon his head, as if in benediction.

It made Quadratus shiver, soldier as he was, to witness this, but it was the usual mode of installing the patriarch of Alexandria; and certainly, Athanasius had been as a dutiful son to his predecessor, and his grief was no false show, for he felt he had lost a friend and father, and likewise knew that in accepting the high office, as his successor, he was but fulfilling Alexander's wish and desire, so that to him the laying on of that dead hand was not a mockery, but a solemn laying upon him of the duties and responsibilities of the holy office, which he was then promising to discharge fully and faithfully.

What it would cost him to be faithful to the vows he was now taking he little dreamed, as he stood before the crowded congregation at the close of the ceremony, no longer an insignificant deacon, but patriarch of the principal Church of Egypt. Could he have looked through the vista of years stretching on before him, and seen the cruel accusations, condemnations, and exile that awaited him because he would not yield to the imperial power in matters of conscience, his heart might have failed him at the prospect; but all this was mercifully hidden from him, and he entered upon his duties with all the ardor of his age and

VISTA: *spreading view*
ARDOR: *passion*

temperament, and Alexandria might well be excused for the pride she felt in her young but noble, blameless and uncompromising young patriarch.

Quadratus went back to his duty with his mind almost at rest concerning Placidia. She must have died in the riot or shortly afterward he felt assured, or she would have been discovered long since. This was the opinion of her sister and all their friends, and so the memory of the young nun and her mysterious disappearance gradually faded, and she ceased to be thought of unless some circumstance brought her to mind again, when her story was told with scarcely more interest than an oft-repeated tale; for the tide of life flowed on as rapidly then as now, and Placidia's place in the Alexandrian world was soon covered and forgotten, while she lived her quiet, lowly, unnoticed life at Antioch, unknown by all save God, who from her quiet, silent ministry of love and service would yet bless the world with an abundant harvest, the fruit of which still stretches on to our own time, and will never be forgotten.

Chapter XI

John Chrysostom

UPWARD of thirty years have passed when we again take up the thread of our story—years of change for the empire and the Church. Constantine and his three sons have all passed away. Cruel and faithless tyrants the latter had proved in spite of their profession of Christianity, and the Church, unable to resist, had too often proved herself an accomplice of those tyrants in the person of her bishops. Constantius, the most unprincipled of these sons, obtained from the Bishop of Nicomedia a forged scroll, purporting to be the last will of Constantine, in which he was made to say that he had been poisoned by the contrivance of his brothers. This was made the pretext for the massacre of two uncles and seven cousins of Constantius without trial.

Gallus and Julian were, with difficulty, saved from the daggers of the assassins. A few years later the weak-minded Gallus was drawn into the commission of deeds that appeared like treason

PURPORTING: *falsely claiming*

against his cousin, who, having survived his brothers, now reigned as sole emperor, and his life was the penalty.

That Julian, now the sole survivor of the Flavian family, should imbibe a hatred against a religion that seemed to sanction these murders was but natural, and though he conformed outwardly to its rites during the lifetime of his cousin, his intimate friends knew that he detested it; and when at length Constantius died, and Julian succeeded to the imperial throne, he threw off all disguise, and declared it to be his intention to restore the worship of the old Olympian deities. The accession of a new emperor was the signal for rejoicing throughout the vast empire, and men thought of little else than shows and spectacles, feasting and merriment.

Antioch, like every other city, indulged in a series of rejoicings, but they were suddenly brought to an end one day by the publication of an edict closing all the schools where Christian instruction was given, which caused dire alarm in many a citizen's household throughout the wealthy Asiatic city.

In the small household of a widow, named Arethusa, whose only son, a lad about fourteen, was in one of the best schools of Antioch, the feeling was not one of disappointment only, but dire alarm, when he went home with the news that the school was closed.

IMBIBE: *absorb*

OLYMPIAN DEITIES: *the Greek gods who, according to Greek mythology, lived on Mount Olympus*

"Placidia," said the widow, addressing an older lady who sat near, "can it be that the persecution, of which thou hast so often told me, is about to be commenced again?"

"Nay, nay, I trust it may not be so, though doubtless the Church hath—"

"Thou art always grumbling about the Church or the monks, Placidia," interrupted the boy. "Now I would rather be a monk than a lawyer," he added, darting a look at his mother as he spoke.

She looked up instantly. "Nay, nay, John; what is there to charm thee in the life of a lazy, illiterate monk," said the lady,

"Lazy—illiterate," repeated the boy.

"Yes; they are of little use to anybody in the world; and many of them are ignorant, as thou knowest," replied his mother.

"But they are holy and devout if they are not learned," said John. "I was talking to a hermit one day, and he told me their manner of life. They rise in the morning wakeful and sober, and, joining together in a choir, they sing with joyful faces and peaceful consciences hymns to the praise of God. They then, on bended knees, implore that God will grant them but one petition—that they may be able to stand with confidence before that dread tribunal when the only Son of God shall come to judge the quick and the dead—that they may never hear those terrible words, 'I know you not.'"[1]

"That is their professed aim and motive I know,

[1] LUKE 13:27

EDICT: *proclamation*

my son, and it is a good one; but not the best—not
the noblest. If all who love the Lord Christ were to
forsake the world and seek only their own salvation, what would become of the men and women
who have not yet learned to love the Lord—what
should I have been better than the pagans thou
dost often laugh at if my Placidia here had become
a nun, as she wished."

"Didst thou wish to be a nun?" asked the boy
curiously. "I thought thou hadst always been my
mother's nurse."

"So I have ever since thy mother needed a nurse.
Thy grandfather bought me in the market here to
take care of her when she was a baby, and I have
never left her since;" and the grave, gentle face
looked lovingly at the young widow, who was as
dear to her as a child is to its mother.

"Thou wert a slave, Placidia!" uttered the boy in
a tone of surprise.

"I am a slave still," said the lady quietly.

But in a moment Arethusa was kneeling at her
side. "Hush, hush, my Placidia," she said; "thou
hast promised to forget this. Thou didst say, when
the parchments were destroyed setting thee free,
that thou wouldst never think of thyself as a slave
again, and now—now thou hast told John," almost
sobbed the lady.

"It will do him no harm, my Arethusa," said Placidia, stroking the soft bands of smoothly braided
hair. "I wanted to tell him of my life in Alexandria,

and how I willfully determined to fly to the desert, until God taught me there was work to be done in the world—work that angels might rejoice to be engaged in," looking fondly in the gentle face she held between her hands.

"I should like to hear about it," said John, seating himself on a cushion at his mother's feet. "How strange it seemeth, Placidia, to hear that thou didst want to be a nun."

"Nay, I was a nun," said Placidia, "and have kept my early vows, only God called me to work in the world instead of allowing me to shut myself up in the desert; and I hope that thou, too, wilt work for the world and not for thyself exclusively, for true and honest men will be needed if our new emperor thinks of crushing out our holy religion."

John made no reply to this, for his heart was set on retiring to a group of hills a few miles from the city where a band of monks had established a monastery.

Arethusa looked uneasily at her son as she saw these thoughts were still working in his mind; but she knew that her faithful friend and nurse would use all her influence to induce the boy to give up this project, and she tried to leave the matter in God's hands, as Placidia advised.

A little later the two friends were talking together by themselves, and Placidia told Arethusa of the anxiety she had for a long time felt when she first came to Antioch lest the Christian religion should die out, as the old Jewess said it would.

"I can smile at the fear now," said Placidia, "and laugh at her assumption of being a prophetess; but it was a very serious thing to me once."

"Then thou dost not think Julian hath the power to put down the Christian faith even if he exalts the pagan worship again," said Arethusa.

"I do not think it is in the power of any emperor to do this, because 'the fullness of time'[1] had come when God sent His Son into the world, and ever since our holy faith hath been making new conquests—spreading its light wider and wider through the world, and it will do so still, although a time of chastening may come upon the Church for her sins and corruptions."

"Her sins!" repeated Arethusa.

"Yes; she hath accommodated herself to the vices and cruelties of those who patronized her, and that Julian should hate all Christians is not surprising."

Arethusa, however, looked her surprise. "Art thou not too harsh, Placidia?"

"Nay, it cannot be too harsh to say that the Church is forgetting her holy mission when her bishops will supply forged wills as the pretext for a number of murders, as the Bishop of Nicomedia did. Thou dost forget that our present emperor barely escaped being massacred with his brothers and uncle, and that he doth lay the sin of these murders on a Christian bishop."

[1] GALATIANS 4:4

Arethusa shivered with horror. "The world is very wicked," she said; "I cannot wonder that John wishes to leave it for a quiet retreat in the hills."

"But John Chrysostom must not leave it," said Placidia solemnly; "he must learn, as I did, that 'God so loved the world that He gave His only begotten Son'[1] to redeem it. It is as wicked now as then; and if it be plain to us to witness its sin, what must it be to Him who is pure and holy. Surely if we are partakers of His love—the love that loved the world—we can share its pain too, and bear with the world for the sake of helping it."

"Such love is certainly nobler than flying from its temptations to secure the salvation of our own souls," said Arethusa.

"Yes, and we must teach John to battle bravely against the evil of the world, but not to fly from it."

It was a delicate task Arethusa had undertaken, and one that gained but little sympathy among her Christian friends; for if a lad gave any indications of piety in those days, it was generally the most earnest wish of parents that he should embrace a monastic life, and John himself greatly desired this, young as he was. The wish was not extraordinary for an earnest, devout mind, sick of the prevailing frivolity and love of sensual pleasure. The wealthy, dissolute Asiatic city had gathered to itself all that was most choice and corrupt of Greek manners and Roman luxury, and these, added to

[1] JOHN 3:16
PIETY: *devotion to God*
DISSOLUTE: *immoral*

the old Syrian stock, grew into an efflorescence of voluptuousness in spite of its being the most important Christian city of Asia, and the first to give the disciples their distinguishing name.[1]

In such a city there was plenty of work for willing hands, and Placidia and Arethusa were both occupied the greater part of the day in visiting the hospital or prison, the poor within the city walls, or the beggars and sick who often lay in the fields outside, for strangers in these conditions were not allowed to pass the gates. To provide for these, and honor the memory of those who had suffered in the persecutions, food was daily carried out and placed upon their tombs, and it was upon this errand Placidia was bent today when she went out after her conversation with Arethusa. The widow herself would remain at home with her son to assist him with his studies, and talk over the advisability of his attending the school of Libanus.

Libanus was one of the last disciples of Plato, and the most learned grammarian and rhetorician of the age, but he was a heathen, and Arethusa was naturally anxious about placing her son under such a master.

John himself looked grave when she made the proposal, but he did not urge any objection, merely saying with a smile, "My mother, we shall defeat the emperor's plans if all do this."

"The emperor's plans!" repeated Arethusa.

[1] Acts 11:26

EFFLORESCENCE OF VOLUPTUOUSNESS: *blossoming of sensual indulgence*

"My mother, hast thou not thought that depriving Christian children of the means of instruction is one of his plans to overturn Christianity? If the children are left to grow up in ignorance it will fall into contempt in a few years, lose its power, and die, while paganism, being upheld by learning and philosophy, will again flourish."

But his mother shook her head. "Nay, nay, John, learning is a helpful handmaid to our holy religion, and I am greatly desirous that being a Christian thou shouldst be a learned man likewise; but do not forget this, my son, that our religion is divine, and not dependent upon philosophy for its continuance."

The lad bowed his head in assent, but still remained thoughtful. "I was not speaking my own thoughts, but what I have heard as being the emperor's design," he said slowly.

"Then, if such be his design, it behooves all Christian parents to see that their children are carefully instructed; and if the schools be closed, our ministers and bishops, and such men as have the gift of knowledge, should be invited to teach them at home or in the chambers of the church."

This mention of the church reminded John of a duty which he and his mother had almost forgotten. He was one of the readers attached to the church, for in those days manuscript copies of the Scriptures being very expensive, and many of the congregation unable to read, it was

GRAMMARIAN: *teacher of grammar*
RHETORICIAN: *teacher of public speaking*

customary for them to assemble in a chamber adjoining the church to hear chapters or portions of it read. So John prepared to go out at once, arranging to meet his mother after the evening service, for there would be a short one tonight in preparation for the full worship of the next day, Friday, for in these early ages Wednesday, Friday, and Sunday, as being typical of the Epiphany, Easter, and Pentecost, were set aside for divine worship. Some there were, of course, who found Sunday quite enough, and others who urged that the Jewish custom of going up to the temple three times a year as the correct orthodox plan, and only presented themselves in the church at the time of the feasts, but, nevertheless, there was always a large congregation.

As John turned into the handsome street and passed under the marble colonnade, he was astonished to see a crowd of people running in the direction of the cathedral, and, following close upon their heels, a party of the city guard apparently in hot pursuit. Anxious to ascertain the cause he hurried after them, and just before the church was gained saw them suddenly stop, and on drawing nearer he discovered that they had captured one of the men of whom they had been in pursuit, but the other had gained the church, and, therefore, could not be touched; for the right of sanctuary had been transferred from the heathen temples to the Christian churches by the order of

EPIPHANY: *the day the Magi came to see Christ*
EASTER: *the day of Christ's resurrection*
PENTECOST: *the day the Holy Spirit was first given*

Constantine, and, though the guards might curse and swear, they dare not approach the altar, where the poor panting wretch who had escaped them was now kneeling.

They led his unfortunate companion off to prison as John ascended the broad marble steps and passed into the outer court, where Jews, pagans, and unbaptized people assembled, and then passed on to the second space, where, beneath the vast dome—emblem of eternity—the congregation of believers sat. The afternoon sun falling upon the jewels set in the walls and colored marble mosaic floor, gave them a warm brilliance beside the snowy marble pillars with their wreaths of beaten gold. But John scarcely glanced at this today, but looked on to the third division of the church, where the bishop's chair stood surrounded by a semicircular seat for the clergy, and beyond, the altar itself, above which there was a statue of Christ, bending forward, as if looking down in tenderest pity upon the trembling fugitive clinging to the rails below.

John wondered whether he had seen this statue as he slowly advanced up the church. No one else was near to point his gaze toward it, and so he timidly advanced and entered the space exclusively set apart for the ministers. Pointing upward with his finger, as he made the sign of the cross, he said, in a gentle voice, "Thou hast escaped through the mercy of Him whom that statue represents, wilt thou not seek from Him the pardon of all thy sins?"

"No!" answered the man. "I reverence Christ as a good and holy being, but Arius taught us better than that we should worship Him now;" and, in spite of the place and circumstances, he drew his robe away from John as though he would contaminate him.

The boy's cheeks flushed angrily for a moment, but he subdued his emotion, and without venturing nearer he said, "Can I do anything for thee?"

"Is he taken—my friend, Victor?"

"Yes, the guards led him away as I came into the church. Can we do anything for him? hast thou friends in Antioch?"

The man shook his head. "We came from Egypt to meet friends, but they are in worse trouble than ourselves. Wilt thou or thy friends go to Victor, in prison, and tell him—tell him?—but there, thou wilt know best what to say, although thou art a Catholic instead of an Arian;" and then the fugitive turned aside his head and groaned. "Leave me now," he said the next minute, "I am safe here;" and so John went slowly down toward the side entrance to the chamber where his little congregation would be waiting to hear him read.

Chapter XII

Beyond the Gates

PLACIDIA passed out of the city gates with her palm-leaf baskets laden with food, and took her way to the tombs of the martyrs, where a crowd of hungry wayfarers were sure to have assembled. As soon as these had been fed from one basket, she took the other to a spot compared with which this field of the dead and desolate was bright and joyous. None but the most brave and fearless among the devoted band of Christian women ever ventured within the dreadful enclosure Placidia was now entering, and anything more gloomy than the aspect of this place could not be imagined. Not a blade of grass was to be seen, not a green leaf stirred in the breeze this soft balmy spring day; the very ground within these barriers looked blighted, and the groups of black tents scattered here and there showed little stir of active life within or without, only a few bent, worn figures of men, crippled, maimed, and blind, creeping and tottering in and out of some of these miserable dwellings.

ASPECT: *appearance*

At the sight of Placidia they looked up with a smile of welcome, for she was as an angel of light to this village of lepers, bringing to them some tidings of home and loved ones, who dared not come near themselves, and bringing to others, who were lonely and desolate and must have starved but for the charity of the Church, food and raiment, and to all the Word of God.

Some within the goats'-hair tents could not lift themselves from their beds, and these Placidia fed with her own hands and spoke such words of comfort as they needed; and round the door of one of the tents, where two or three of the most helpless were lying, the rest would gather, carefully covering their mouths as they drew near, that the poison of their breath should not fall upon the visitor. It was wonderful to think how she had passed in and out among them for years, spending hours sometimes in that poisonous atmosphere, and yet had never taken this dreadful Eastern pestilence. She certainly took all the precautions possible, sitting always in the tent door to read, and her auditors, if they wished to speak, stood at some distance and not directly facing her; yet still she knew, and they knew, that each time she came it might be the last as their visitor and ministering angel, and that she might have to take up her abode among them for the rest of her days as the result of her devoted love. Hitherto, however, she had escaped, almost by a miracle as it seemed to her, but she

PESTILENCE: *disease*

was careful after leaving this lazar village to walk a long way in the outskirts before venturing to enter the city again or approach any of her friends. Arethusa she never allowed to come near this spot. Her life must be protected for her son's sake, she insisted, and so the young widow had yielded and let her follow this work alone.

To avoid speaking to anyone while on her return from the lepers was Placidia's great care, and today, when she saw a woman approaching, she passed over to the other side of the road. To her annoyance, however, the woman crossed too, and as she drew nearer Placidia saw that she looked worn and weary, and her clothes, which had once been rich and costly, were now shabby, frayed, and travel-stained.

"Nay, nay; do not bid me depart until I have spoken," she said. "I am poor, old, and hungry, but if I can only reach Antioch I am safe."

"Thou hast friends, then, in the city?" asked Placidia, strangely moved by the manner and voice of the poor stranger.

"Yes, my brother is there, or will be there shortly; he has been to the war in Persia."

"But the Persian war is over, and Constantius is dead," said Placidia.

"Dead—dead!" whispered the stranger, looking as though she could not credit the intelligence.

"Yes, he died some weeks since, and his cousin, Julian, is our emperor now."

LAZAR: *someone with leprosy, from the man Lazarus in one of Jesus' parables who was covered with sores*
CREDIT: *believe*

"And the army—the guard of the labarum—they are at Antioch still?"

Placidia shook her head. "Where hast thou been lately not to have heard of the death of Constantius, and that Julian hath declared himself a pagan?" she asked.

But instead of replying the woman sank to the ground with a deep groan, murmuring, "Not at Antioch! not at Antioch! and they told me I should find him there."

"Whom didst thou wish to find?" asked Placidia, gently raising and supporting her.

"My brother; he is one of the sacred guard, and they are not at Antioch thou sayest."

"No, they have not been at Antioch since our emperor started on his expedition to Persia. But hast thou no other friends?" she asked.

"I am a widow and have but one son, and he is at Tagaste, in Numidia."

"And thou camest from Tagaste?" asked Placidia, looking more curiously at the stranger.

"Nay, nay; I came from Alexandria on a pilgrimage to Jerusalem, and dwelt there some years, until the Jews robbed me of all I possessed, and then I started for Antioch to meet my brother as he went to Persia, but was taken ill at Damascus and lay in the hospital many weeks. Then they told me I should meet him as he returned, but I have been a long time on the journey and now I am too late—thou art sure I am too late?" she added questioningly.

"Yes, the emperor's guard is not there now. But I came from Alexandria," said Placidia, "and long to hear of friends I left there, so if thou wilt return with me I can give thee food and shelter, and the next messenger that journeys to Tagaste or Constantinople might carry a letter to thy son or brother."

The stranger's face brightened at the kind offer, but for a minute or two she could only press Placidia's hand in token of her gratitude as she took her arm for support. "The God of my martyred father wilt bless thee for thy kindness to a stranger," she managed to say at last.

Placidia started at the words "My father, too, was a martyr," she said impulsively; then noticing how weak and spent her companion seemed, she hastily added, "but do not talk of this or anything else now, we have still a long walk to the city gates, and—"

"But I am destitute, and they tell me I shall not be admitted," interrupted the stranger, trembling with apprehension.

"Leave that to me," said Placidia confidently. "I am known to the guard and he will not turn thee back."

The stranger made no reply beyond a grateful pressure of the hand as she glanced down at her travel-stained dress. It had been very handsome once—its gold threads worked into a representation of Christ's miracle of feeding five thousand.

There might not be as many figures as this, but
there they sat in little crowds still, headless, arm-
less, and in a general state of dilapidation from
the fraying of the gold threads; but the larger-
sized upright figures of Christ and his disciples,
that occupied the back of the robe, were in a better state of preservation, and the dress, shabby
as it was, gave its wearer a stately air still, and
convinced Placidia that she was a lady at least.
What other thoughts the sight of the stranger had
stirred within her she carefully concealed, but she
was very gentle and considerate toward her as they
slowly made their way toward the gate of the city.
The outer one was passed without difficulty, but
the guard posted at the inner gate looked at them
curiously as they crossed the bridge spanning the
deep ditch running between the inner and outer
walls, and as Placidia drew near with her companion leaning on her arm, he said questioningly,
"Sick?"

"No," answered Placidia, "only travel-worn and
weary from a long journey," and she stepped forward and whispered something in an undertone
that appeared to satisfy the man, although he
looked surprised as he glanced from one to the
other.

They had still a long distance to walk for one
so weak and weary, for Placidia lived on the outskirts of the city, close to where the rushing Orontes tumbled its turbid waters along toward the

DILAPIDATION: *decay or ruin*
TURBID: *turbulent*

sea. Any doubt of the stranger being welcomed by
Arethusa never crossed Placidia's mind, for it was
almost as mother and daughter that they had lived
for years now.

By the time they reached home people were
preparing to go to church; but Placidia had no intention of leaving the stranger to the care of the
servants. She directed them to prepare a meal
at once, and then leading her visitor to her own
room, she took off her shoes, helped her to un-
robe, and after she had taken some refreshment,
led her to the bath that had been prepared for
her, laying out at the same time the best robe she
possessed for the stranger to put on, as well as all
other things she would require. When this was
all over, and the stranger comfortably placed on
a couch by the window overlooking the Orontes,
Placidia came and sat down beside her.

"Wilt thou tell me something of Alexandria
—canst thou tell me now?" she said a little eagerly. "Thou saidst thy father was a martyr, and
I thought—I thought—" Placidia's breath was coming in quick gasps, but she subdued her emotion,
for the stranger was looking at her curiously.

For a minute or two the stranger did not speak,
but sat looking fixedly at her, until at last she said,
"Thou dost remind me strangely of a sister I lost a
long time since."

"Thirty-four years ago?" said Placidia. "Melissa!
my sister! dost thou not know me?" she added,

throwing her arms around her sister's neck. "Hast thou forgotten Placidia—little Placidia, as thou wert wont to call me?"

"Placidia!" repeated Melissa, slowly passing her hand across her forehead, as though she feared her mind was wandering. "Placidia was a nun," she said, looking at her sister's simple, but not conventual dress.

"Placidia is a nun still in this, that she labors for God in the way He hath directed her, though not in the way she wished," said her sister slowly.

Melissa raised herself, and looked again in her sister's face, and the next minute she uttered a short scream as she threw herself into her arms. "Yes, yes; I know thee now," she sobbed. "I saw my father in thine eyes. Fool that I was not to recognize thee before, only I thought—I thought—"

"I was dead," whispered Placidia through her tears, "while I have often thought of Melissa, and saw my mother in thy face soon after I met thee."

"Thou didst often think of me," said Melissa, suddenly looking up, "and yet thou hast never written, never sent to tell me of thy safety. O, Placidia, my sister, how couldst thou treat us thus cruelly! for both Quadratus and I went in search of thee after the riot."

"Quadratus," repeated Placidia; "thou meanest Lucullus, thy husband."

"Lucullus made every inquiry possible," said Melissa; "but Quadratus went in search of thee

WONT: *accustomed*
CONVENTUAL DRESS: *the dress of a convent*

through the desert, and was the last to give up hope of seeing thee again."

"Then he was not killed in that dreadful riot! The slaves told me he was, or—or— O, Melissa, if I had known he had escaped I think I should have written to thee after I came to Antioch—I could not have done so before."

"And why didst thou not, my Placidia! Thou knewest thou hadst a sister who loved thee," said Melissa reproachfully.

"I was not sure that thou didst love me in those days. I had tried to crush every human love out of my own heart, and—and I was filling it with pride instead—spiritual pride, which is the worst of all. I thought myself better than thee or Lucullus, or even my dear, holy mother. Nay, nay; do not hinder me. I must tell thee this now, how I was mistaken and puffed up, and yet—yet I did want to serve God, Melissa."

"I am sure thou didst, my Placidia!"

"Only it was in the wrong way," went on Placidia. "I thought myself too good for common everyday use in the world. I, the child of a martyr, must do something different from that, and so to go to the desert and leave a name in Alexandria for holiness and devotion became the desire of my heart, and everything and everybody was sacrificed for it, and I grew proud and scornful."

"Nay, nay, my Placidia, speak not so harshly of thyself."

Placidia shook her head, and smiled. "I am only calling things by their right names now," she said; "I did not call it pride and scorn then, but I have since learned to know that it was."

"But thou hast not told me why thou didst not write to us," interrupted Melissa.

"Canst thou ask—canst thou wonder that I felt doubtful about applying to thee or Lucullus after the way I treated thee at home, more especially as I had no chance of doing so until nearly a year afterward, when I was brought here and sold."

"Sold!" repeated Melissa, with a start of horror. "Placidia, do not tell me thou hast been a slave," she said, covering her face with her hands, while the tears ran down between her fingers.

"Nay, nay, Melissa; do not grieve at God's way of granting my wish, it was the best way after all," she added.

Melissa drew her sister nearer to her. "O, my Placidia, I cannot bear to think of it while I was re-pining and murmuring in the midst of luxury—"

"I was saved all that trouble and care by having plenty of work to do—the homely work of washing and dressing little children, and teaching them what I could of the love of God in Christ Jesus our Lord."

"And then thou didst marry, Placidia?"

"Nay, I might, perhaps, but for my early vows," said the sister with a slight blush. "My nun's dress had been torn from me, it is true, but they could not touch my heart, and, besides, I had placed myself under the protection of my vows to save myself from—from a fate worse than death; and, after that, how could I break them?"

"But thou art not a slave now," said Melissa, looking round the pleasant, elegantly-furnished room in which they sat.

"I am, and I am not. Arethusa is my daughter and my mistress too," said Placidia, with a smile, and then she explained her meaning, and again begged for news of her brother and Alypus, and how she came to leave Alexandria.

"I was driven away when our brave patriarch, Athanasius, fled to the desert. Thou dost remember his struggle with Arius, and how he hath opposed his doctrine even against the late emperor, who was an Arian. Thou hast, doubtless, heard too how Constantius tried to get rid of him because he withstood his assumption to control the Church in all things, and appointed in his place George of Cappadocia, an Arian like himself, to rule over the Church of Alexandria. It was one Thursday night in February when this evil man entered the church where we were gathered for service, and ordered the guards he had brought with him to seize Athanasius as he sat in his chair. But at this word the congregation rose and begged the patriarch to save his life by flight. This, however, he would not do until nearly all the people had left, and then he quietly passed out and made his way to the desert of Thebes, where he hath dwelt ever since; building up the faith of the Church by his writings, now that he is no longer able to preach."

"And this Arian bishop, George," said Placidia, "evil tidings have been brought to us concerning him."

"Not more evil than he himself is, for he is a shepherd who sheareth the sheep but never feedeth them. He came to our city with the state of a barbarian conqueror, and, like a cruel oppressor, he laid heavy taxes upon our merchants, until they were fain to leave or give up all thought of trading. My Lucullus died shortly afterward, and Alypus carried what he could of our possessions to Tagaste, for the heavy duties on salt, niter, and other things were consuming our substance, and the last tax was more vexatious than any, for he founded it on the right of the old Pharaohs of Egypt to all the houses in the city, and laid a tax upon them."

"And this was done by a Christian bishop, under a Christian emperor!" exclaimed Placidia sadly. "Melissa, a time of purging is at hand I feel sure, and it may be the martyrs are not all buried yet."

NITER: *potassium nitrate, used for salting meat*

Chapter XIII

A Day in Antioch

A RETHUSA and her son welcomed Melissa almost as warmly as Placidia had done, but John seemed a little disappointed, too, when he saw how ill their visitor looked, and how much occupied Placidia was with her sister. He hardly liked to mention the promise he had made to the fugitive in the church now, and yet the prisoner ought to be visited, and there was no time to lose, for he had no doubt but that there were, here in Antioch, some of the conspirators concerned in the plot for which the Proconsul of Africa and the Prefect of Egypt were condemned to be executed.

Placidia soon noticed the boy's perplexed and anxious looks, and before retiring for the night she asked him if he had heard any fresh news, for her mind was full of the story her sister had told her concerning the oppression and tyranny of the patriarch, George, of Alexandria.

John shook his head. "It is no news that a fugitive took refuge in the church," he said, "and that his companion was taken to prison."

"Who were they?" asked Placidia.

"Strangers in Antioch, and I have promised that thou shouldst visit this prisoner," said John dubiously.

"I will go in the morning," said Placidia quietly.

"But thy sister—" suggested John.

"She will be better, doubtless; she is but weary with long travel, and I have let her talk too much for her feeble strength."

So at sunrise the next morning Placidia, with her palm-leaf basket, containing the prisoner's breakfast, was outside the gates of the prison, waiting for the gloomy portal to unclose and admit her, as well as several others, bound on the same mission of mercy.

She was silently shown to where the African prisoner was secured, and then the warden left her to make his acquaintance by herself, while he passed on with another visitor. Placidia had become accustomed to the gloom of the place, and saw that an old man, white-haired and bowed with age, sat on the ground before her. "I am sorry to see thee in this evil case," she said compassionately, taking some honey-cakes from her basket as she spoke.

The old man lifted his head and looked at her. "Thou art one of the pillars of the Church," he said in a sneering tone without noticing her gift.

Placidia started as she heard the clear ringing tones of his voice. Where had she heard it before;

PORTAL: *door, gate*

why did it cause her to start and tremble with some undefined sense of horror? She looked at him again more earnestly, and he looked at her, but there was no recognition in his face.

"Thou art one of the pillars of the Church," he said; "the fanatical Church that our new emperor will crush out of existence. I belonged to it once— was a Catholic and then an Arian, and now I am going back to the old faith of Greece and Rome, and will help Julian to restore Apollo to his shrine of Daphne, if he will only let me live. O, to be at Carthage once more when the old worship and the old games are restored!"

At the mention of Carthage Placidia started. In a moment the half-drunken flower-crowned prefect rose before her in the place of this old man. "Thou wert prefect of Carthage once," she said as quietly as she could.

"Ah! thou knowest me, then," said the old man.

"I did know thee. Dost thou remember old Deborah, the Jewess, and—"

"And Onias, her kinsman, thou wouldst say," interrupted the prisoner. "Thou, then, art in possession of their secrets, but I tell thee, as I told him, I will have nothing to do with the Jews or their accursed temple either. I know them too well, for if it had not been for them and their money-lending I should not be here," and he spat at his visitor in the impotence of his rage.

"I am no Jewess," said Placidia calmly, "I am a

IMPOTENCE: *powerlessness*

simple Christian woman, who would fain do thee good if thou wilt allow me."

But the old man shook his head. "Ye Christians can do me no good," he said scornfully. "I tell thee I have renounced thy faith; send me a priest of the old worship if thou wilt, and tell Onias, the Jew, he had better apply to the emperor to build his temple and overthrow the Church of the Resurrection that stands on Calvary, where a temple of Venus once stood."

Placidia shuddered as she looked at the white-haired old man as he said these bitter, mocking words. "The emperor would not—" she began.

"The emperor will do that or anything else. He hates this faith as much as I do," angrily interposed the prisoner.

Placidia saw it would be useless to attempt anything like an appeal to his conscience this morning, and so she silently put down the food she had brought, and with a word of farewell departed.

The streets were crowded by this time, and the bells ringing for church. Arethusa and John would be waiting for her, and so she hurried home with her basket, still feeling anxious and perturbed from her interview with the prisoner. She was not so fully occupied, however, as to pass unnoticed the change in some of the ladies' dresses this morning. New and strange the devices looked to her, but they were ominous tokens, too, of the change that might come over the Christian Church; for it

INTERPOSED: *interrupted*

was no mere caprice of fashion that had embroidered the chase of Diana on the shawls and robes, and substituted the grasshopper of Pallas Athene for the cross and dove.

The Jews, too, seemed to be unusually busy, or else it was Placidia's fancy, weaving fears out of what she had heard in the prison concerning them and the emperor.

The sight of Arethusa and John, however, roused her from this unusual despondency, and on hearing that Arethusa had just seen Melissa, and left her quite comfortable, she put down her basket and set off to church with them.

Fashionable Antioch was divided now between churchgoing and attending the old games in the theater and arena; but the majority still went to the cathedral services, and a long line of litters, with blue or pink silk hangings, and borne on poles, inlaid with gold or ivory, were setting down their occupants near the church steps. A female slave was usually in attendance upon these ladies, and, as they stepped from their litters, placed a pair of slippers over their jeweled sandals and arranged their embroidered silk robes or shawls in graceful folds. Very quaint and gaudy were some of these dresses, with their representations of the miracles or scenes from the lives of the martyrs, in many colored embroidery of silk, with borders of crosses or doves. Everyone wore a cross, and carried a small roll of the Scriptures, clasped with jewels,

CAPRICE: *sudden impulse*
CHASE: *hunt*
PALLAS ATHENE: *the Greek goddess of wisdom*

and attached to a necklace of gold or pearls, and it was no uncommon sight to see these richly attired ladies fall upon their knees and kiss the hem of some passing monk's garment, and meekly implore their blessing.

As Placidia and Arethusa were about to ascend the church steps this morning they were delayed by a little crowd of these ladies so kneeling, while their slaves in attendance still stood near the litters, not venturing to approach too near.

With a single glance John Chrysostom took in the whole scene, and his pale, earnest face flushed as he said in a passionate whisper, "I wish I was a monk, I would rebuke this false humility. I would tell these ladies to deal more kindly with their slaves instead of kissing my garments."

"Hush! hush!" whispered his mother; "do not talk of being a monk; we need Christian lawyers and magistrates more than monks now." This disputed point was dropped by the ladies rising from their knees, and thus clearing the church steps so that they could pass into their accustomed places.

When they returned home Placidia went at once to Melissa's room, and found that she had risen from her couch, and was kneeling before a small cross which she had placed on a pedestal the night previous. Placidia had not noticed it then, but she saw now that it was inlaid with wood and encased in crystal, and that Melissa kept her eyes reverently fixed upon it as she prayed.

Placidia gazed an instant at her sister and was about to leave the room again, when Melissa rose from her knees, and after kissing the little cross, held it toward Placidia as she begged her to return. "Take it, my sister," she said, "it is the most precious relic a Christian can possess."

"What is it?" asked Placidia curiously.

"The wood of the true cross. A portion of it was sent to the new capital of the empire, Constantinople, by the empress-mother, Helena, but some is still in the Church of the Resurrection, and the bishop hath had some encased in gold and jewels, that pilgrims may take this with them to all lands in memory of our Lord and Master."

"But if the true cross is thus cut up and carried away by pilgrims there will be nothing left of it soon," said Placidia, gazing at the slip of wood in its golden case.

"Nay, but, my sister, this wood of the true cross is like the widow's cruse of oil, it is a never-failing miracle, for in spite of so much being taken away it never grows less—never decreases in size or weight."

Placidia looked doubtful. "Didst thou hear this at Jerusalem, Melissa?" she asked.

"It is a well-known fact at Jerusalem," she said quickly; "how else could the bishop sell so many of these precious relics?"

How, indeed, but by imposing on the ignorance and superstition of those who thought it was a meritorious work to visit the tombs of the martyrs and the place where their Lord had lived and died.

Placidia recalled the day when she had stood with old Deborah on the slope of the hill overlooking the little colony that had gathered round the sacred mount of Calvary and watched the procession of monks as they carried the lately exhumed cross, and for the first time a faint doubt crept into her mind as to whether this was the true cross after all—whether it had not been placed there by some monk who afterward took care to lead Helena to where it might be found. She almost hated herself for the thought, and yet she had seen so much of worldliness and self-seeking pride and arrogance under a show of humility in this city of Antioch, which yet gloried in the name of Christian, that she could not so fully believe in the miracles and wonders in which she once had such unquestioning faith.

From this reverie over the little cross, which she still held, she was aroused by Melissa asking if they had any statues of the saints or virgin-mother in the house. For a minute or two Placidia could scarcely comprehend her meaning until she recalled the splendid household at Alexandria, and Alypus telling her one day that the Venus standing in Melissa's chamber was the mother of the Lord Jesus—the mother of love and the guardian of the heart. She had been half-vexed, half-amused then at what she attributed to Melissa's fertile fancy,

MERITORIOUS: *praiseworthy*
EXHUMED: *dug up*

but she looked more serious now. "The saints or virgin-mother," she repeated.

"Yes, I have missed them sorely since I have left Alexandria," said Melissa, "and I thought—"

"But surely thou dost not worship these, my sister," said Placidia.

"No, not worship them, but—but they help me greatly, Placidia. I told Quadratus once of the difficulty I felt in remembering always the love and sympathy of the Lord Christ and—"

"Did he tell thee that the statues of the old demon-gods would bring that love to thy mind?" interrupted Placidia.

Melissa shook her head. "He did not like the statues being retained in our household," she said. "It was a woman from Thrace whom Lucullus bought to nurse Alypus, who told me how it helped her to understand the love of the Lord Christ—to think of the love and tenderness of His mother. She had a little statue of Venus, which she placed in her chamber to help her think of this when she prayed, and I would fain have one, too, for I have sorely missed it since I have been journeying."

Placidia knew not what to say to these strange words of her sister's. She had heard that some of the people of Thrace had placed the statues of Venus and Juno beside that of the Saviour, calling them the mother of the Lord, and holding them in almost equal reverence; but that Melissa should do this, in the midst of enlightened Alexandria, was a puzzle indeed. What could she say against its use either if, as her sister said, it helped her to comprehend the love of Christ, for she knew what her own difficulties had been in this direction under the teaching of Athanasius.

But there was not a statue in the house she knew, and she felt thankful that she could say so now, for she was by no means easy in her own mind as to this bowing before the old gods, it was too much like idolatry—too much like breaking the express command concerning graven images and their worship—and she ventured to tell Melissa this a few days afterward, for it was settled that she should remain at Antioch for the present, as there was some talk of the emperor visiting the city in the course of the summer, and if he came Quadratus would be sure to come with him, the sisters argued, and both were anxious to see him.

Meanwhile Placidia continued her work of visiting the lepers and the prison as usual, but she made very little impression on the old man, Victor. He was still detained, but had every liberty possible, although his fellow-conspirators had been executed, and his guards said he deserved a similar punishment, only his well-known leaning toward paganism had saved him. His fate would not be decidedly known until the emperor came himself to Antioch, when it was expected the old temples would be reopened with great splendor.

Everybody in the city was talking of this coming visit, but men laughed at the idea of reviving the old worn-out idolatry. Julian might resuscitate the games of the arena, and they were willing enough to go to the theater; but to believe the old legends of the Olympian divinities was asking too much, now that the light of Christianity had been shed abroad. Ladies changed the fashion of their dresses and wore golden grasshoppers, in honor of Pallas Athene; the men drank a little more and crowned their brows with vine leaves, for the sake of Bacchus; but more than this the imperial edict could not do. A hundred cattle a day were slaughtered in Constantinople, it was rumored, and the emperor's guards, who had sprinkled incense to Jupiter, had a continual feast, but Antioch was not at all disposed to follow this example. Some spectacle in honor of the old deities must be prepared when the emperor came, but cattle and splendid birds were too costly to be thrown away for nothing, and so the change of religion, as a national or state business, made little difference at Antioch for some time.

At length it was known that in June the emperor might confidently be expected, and as the time drew near there was a bustle of preparation for his coming. It was not to be a mere visit of pleasure, however, for he was about to renew the war with Persia, being assured of success by the augurs of Mars and Jupiter, so that his stay might be

RESUSCITATE: *bring back to life*
DIVINITIES: *gods*

prolonged through the winter if all things were not favorable for the campaign to be commenced at once. This brought renewed hope that Quadratus might be in the imperial train, and Placidia and Melissa looked forward with anxious impatience to this meeting with their brother.

Chapter XIV

The Shrine of Daphne

THE tidings came at last that Julian was within a few miles of Antioch, and would enter the city the following morning, and John Chrysostom hearing the news hastened home to tell Placidia, for she and Melissa, as well as his mother, had determined to join the procession of Christians who were going out to meet and welcome him. They had each been busy preparing festive robes for this occasion, for Arethusa had resolved to put off her widow's dress for once, and she and Placidia would wear dresses embroidered with the miracle of Christ raising Lazarus from the dead, while Melissa wore one still more splendid in colors, but repeating the same fact.

John would walk with the readers and collectors of the church, who, with the bishop at their head, in his splendid robes, and a long train of ecclesiastics and monks from the neighboring hills, hoped to disarm the emperor's prejudices by this display of loyalty. The Jews, too, had been making active

DISARM: *overcome*

preparations to welcome the emperor, while those who followed the old paganism would also muster in full force today, so that Antioch was in a state of excitement not often seen.

But to the surprise of Arethusa and her friends, who left home just after sunrise to proceed to the church, they met several people dressed in deep mourning, and as they went on these mourning robes grew more frequent, while the wearers cast wondering but angry glances at the splendid dresses worn by the little party of Christians. John, being at the school of Libanus, the great teacher of rhetoric, knew some of these as friends of his master, and after passing one of the groups he exclaimed, "What can it mean, my mother? these are pagans, I know, and our emperor hath restored their religion, and yet they go forth to meet him with mourning robes." Arethusa shook her head, greatly puzzled. Placida, however, scarcely noticed anything; she could only think of her brother, whom she had long mourned as dead, and was even more impatient than Melissa for the procession to move from the church.

At last, with hymns of alleluia, they set forward on their stately march through the streets toward the gate by which Julian would enter, which was some distance from the church.

Their way lay past the great temple of Jupiter, and as they drew near they saw a crowd collected around a lofty ivory car, everyone wearing a

MUSTER: *assemble*
CAR: *chariot*

mourning robe, and throwing ashes on his head. Little girls dressed in white, and carrying miniature gardens in baskets, stood round the car, but all the flowers in the baskets were drooping and faded, while on the ivory couch lay the dead Adonis. Slowly the Christians comprehended the whole scene—it was the mourning of Adonis, emblem of the sun, and the fading flowers were to typify the languishing earth when the sun was in eclipse. Soft strains of mournful music accompanied the car, while behind came white-robed priests, with rent garments and ashes on their heads, and then the worshipers in mourning robes.

As the procession from the church came up the car moved on, but it was impossible with such a concourse of people to prevent the two processions falling into one if they were to meet the emperor at the city gates, and so with much angry grumbling the Christians halted, drawing their dresses round them, as if fearing contamination, whenever one belonging to the other procession approached too near.

"Placidia, we will go back," whispered Arethusa; "this is no place for Christians, unless they would be partakers in idolatry;" and so, quietly leaving their places, they retraced their steps homeward, leaving John to follow the command of the bishop whether to go on or return to the church.

The sisters were greatly disappointed, but it was the only thing they could do at present, and so

RENT: *torn*
CONCOURSE: *crowd*

the flower-wreathed ivory car passed on toward
the gate to welcome the emperor, while the Christians turned back to the church and bewailed that
Julian had forsaken the faith he had professed and
become an apostate.

The emperor was pleased with the devotion of
his subjects to the service of the gods, but he could
not fail to notice that not a Christian was to be seen
in the streets to bid him welcome. But those who
pressed forward most eagerly with their greetings
were offended at his rough manners, his unkempt,
tangled hair and beard, and his simple mode of
dressing. No dainty, curled, and perfumed sybarite was Julian, but one who, in practice as well as
in name, desired to be a philosopher and a devoted follower of the Greek divinities; and so the gay,
luxurious Antiochians soon grew tired of trying
to please him, and followed their own pleasures
without reference to their imperial visitor.

Day by day Melissa went out with her sister in
the hope of seeing some of the guards of the labarum; but the cross, as the distinctive badge of
the famous guard, had been abolished, and the
Roman eagle once more took its place as of old, so
that the sisters were puzzled to know whether these
standard-bearers were in the emperor's train, or
were left behind to follow with the main body of
the army. Nothing was seen or heard of Quadratus, and when the excitement of the emperor's arrival had begun to wear away, and no tidings came

APOSTATE: *someone who has abandoned his faith*
SYBARITE: *someone devoted to pleasure*

of their brother, Melissa announced her intention of returning to Alexandria or of joining Alypus at Tagaste.

"But thou must not go until thou hast seen the tomb of our martyr-bishop, Babylas, at Daphne," said John, who was present when she announced her intention to Arethusa.

"Nay, indeed, thou must see the groves of Daphne, where my husband is buried and where I hope to be laid," said the widow. "Would it not be possible to spend a few days at the village, Placidia? the change of air would strengthen thy sister for her journey."

"I might leave the city for a few days," said Placidia, a little wearily. She felt the disappointment of not meeting her brother very keenly, and it had begun to tell upon her health. The watchful eyes of Arethusa had noticed this change, and she was anxious to take her away from the city for a short time, where everything reminded her of her recent disappointment. The emperor would not be at Daphne, he had so much business to transact just now, and the hated name of Julian, the apostate, might be forgotten.

So the little household removed to the village of Daphne, about five miles off, where the groves of laurel and cypress cradled the little rills and springs that fed the Orontes, and where, in the fiercest noontide heat of that eastern summer, lone spots might be found so cool and shady, that

RILLS: *streams*

the velvet moss upon the ground was as fresh and green as if watered by a perennial fountain.

These almost impenetrable groves had been the scene of many a wild orgy in the days when Apollo was worshiped by the gay Antiochians, but his shrine was almost deserted now, and the dust of Christian martyrs and confessors had made the place sacred to hundreds of the citizens, a few of whom had settled on the borders of the grove, and thus a village had sprung up, which was often resorted to by those who wanted to get away from the noise and bustle of the city for a time.

Arethusa, therefore, had little difficulty in finding accommodation, but she heard to her dismay that the feast of Apollo was at hand, and that the emperor was expected to worship at the ancient shrine. That half Antioch would follow him was likewise expected; but on the morning of the festival, when the first beams of the rising sun were gilding the tops of the trees, a small company was seen approaching, and, at the same time, an old priest in white robes, with a gray goose under his arm, made his way through the village street, and took the path toward the famous shrine.

As the little company drew nearer, Arethusa recognized Julian by his long unkempt beard; but there were no lines of garlanded cattle or eager worshipers from the city, only a few guards in attendance upon the imperial pontiff, who looked round every now and then as if expecting something or someone to appear. But nothing came,

PERENNIAL: *continual*
PONTIFF: *high priest*

JULIAN AT THE SHRINE OF DAPHNE

and the little company went on to the shrine, where Apollo, cut from the purest marble, was bending over, pouring out a libation upon the earth. Everything around spoke of neglect and desertion, except where the white marble of the Christians' tombs gleamed between the dark foliage of the laurel and cypress. Arethusa and John had gone to visit the tomb of the martyr-bishop, Babylas, and from the slight elevation could see the little company gathered around the shrine, and the poor old priest coming forward with the best offering he could afford—the gray goose. "What!" exclaimed Julian, "hast thou nothing for the divine Apollo but that poor common bird. Where are the cattle and the worshipers?"

The old man shook his head mournfully. "The Christians take all the cattle to feed the poor," he said; "and as for worshipers, none come to this sacred shrine now."

Julian frowned. "I thought I had established the old faith," he said, "but I find the altars everywhere deserted."

"If the loyal citizens of Antioch had known their imperial pontiff desired to officiate at the altar of Apollo they would doubtless have had all things made ready," suggested his trusty friend Alypus, anxious to calm his rising anger.

"But such service would have been for the emperor, not for the god," said Julian; "that was why I kept my determination to visit this shrine a secret from all, for I would fain know whether men had

LIBATION: *an offering of wine*

returned to their old allegiance, and now what do I see—this most sacred spot, that should be tended with all care, dirty, weed-grown, and deserted, one old priest instead of a thousand devout worshipers, and a poor gray goose, to represent the gratitude of the wealthiest city in Asia."

"But that is not the worst, most noble Julian," the old priest ventured to say. "This shrine is not only neglected, but profaned by the dead bodies of those infamous Christians. Their bishop, Babylas, was the first buried at Daphne, but his grave was scarcely closed before others were brought to be laid beside him, and now many are brought every week from Antioch." As he spoke he pointed to where Arethusa and her son were still carefully tending the graves of friends and relatives, who had been laid to rest in this sequestered spot, and the next minute the leafy screen surrounding it was rudely pulled aside, and a party of the imperial guard, led by the old priest, leaped through the gap and went at once to the bishop's grave.

To pull down the tomb which loving hands had raised to his memory was the work of a very few minutes; and while John and his mother stood almost transfixed with horror, the body of the aged martyr was dragged out and thrown into a neglected corner, and the rest of the graves trampled upon, and the tombs broken and defaced.

The widow made her escape as soon as she could, and returned to the village; and as soon as

PROFANED: *defiled*
INFAMOUS: *detestable*
SEQUESTERED: *secluded*

John had seen her safely home he set off to Antioch to inform the bishop and his friends of what had taken place at Daphne, anger lending swiftness to his feet, so that the five miles were traversed and the bishop informed of all the circumstances before midday. Before nightfall every Christian in Antioch had heard of it, and had gone forward to meet the car that had been sent out to convey the body to the city. Every street was crowded with eager, angry people, pressing on behind the long line of monks and church choristers, who met the car at the city gates singing, "All the gods of the nations are idols, but the Lord made the heavens."[1] Defiance was hurled at the emperor in the songs of David, the bishop and presbyters riding on white mules near the car, and selecting those that should be sung as they passed through the street.

Placidia shook her head when she heard of the triumphant display. "I am glad thou hast returned, John," she said, "for I am afraid we have not seen the end of this business yet."

"Nay, but what wouldst thou have us do, Placidia," demanded John.

"Julian is our emperor, as thou knowest."

"Nay, but thou wouldst not have us worship Apollo at the bidding of the emperor," said the lad. "I—I should not wonder if this shrine were destroyed by a miracle after what has happened."

"Nay, my John, talk not so rashly," said his mother; "it is well thou hast left Antioch, or that ready

[1] PSALM 96:5

CHORISTERS: *choir members*

tongue might bring trouble upon all of us;" and it was arranged that they should prolong their stay at Daphne instead of returning the next day, as they had intended.

It was well they had made this arrangement, for the events of the following night were fraught with consequences that few anticipated, and would have made John's incautious words more than ever dangerous if they had been overheard. The night was very hot, and even here in Daphne there was scarcely a breath of air stirring the leaves. Placidia, who was very restless, rose from her couch soon after midnight and opened the little casement of her room to admit more air, and as she did so a bright, luminous ball of fire appeared to dart across the sky in the direction of the famous shrine. Looking earnestly, she soon saw flames and smoke curling upward toward the star-studded heavens, and in a moment John's words recurred to her mind, for she knew at once that it was on fire.

The whole village was soon astir, but there was no hope of saving the matchless statue of Apollo; and when the sun rose the whole shrine was a blackened heap of ruins.

Doubtless many in Antioch rejoiced when they heard what had happened; but the songs of triumph in which they celebrated it were soon stifled by the sighs and groans of anxious alarm, for whatever they might believe as to the cause of the fire, Julian accused them of having done it, and at once

FRAUGHT: *filled*
CASEMENT: *window*

proceeded to find out, if possible, the actual culprit. It needed but this to set his smoldering anger in a blaze of persecution, and now many a peaceful citizen in Antioch, whose only crime was singing the Psalms of David when the body of Babylas was brought into the city, found himself in prison, and his goods carried off to pay the taxes imposed for the support of paganism.

The church itself was almost stripped likewise, for many of the ornaments had been taken from the pagan temple, and now had to be restored, as well as the building itself, at the sole cost of the Christian Church. In vain the bishop pleaded for his flock. Julian pointed with a mocking smile to the costly gold chains and jeweled trappings of his white mule, and told him to learn the blessedness of poverty on which he so often preached, and truly it did seem that the Church needed the lesson just now.

Arethusa, in her quiet retreat of Daphne, heard of all these troubles, and would fain have returned to her city home and taken her share of affliction with the rest; but Placidia and John together persuaded her to remain where she was. She could still pay her quota of the heavy taxes, and help support those who needed the bounty of the Church, and to do this would be of far more use than to place herself in needless danger.

Chapter XV

The Victory of the Vanquished

SLOWLY the days dragged on in the quiet little village of Daphne, where Arethusa and her family still lingered, for they knew not but that they might be seized and thrown into prison if they ventured to return to the city. The cathedral was closed and the public worship of God suspended, while long lines of garlanded cattle might be seen every morning slowly passing through the streets toward the temple of Jupiter for sacrifice.

John was the only one to bring them any news of what was going on in the city, for he generally contrived to obtain some information each day in his wanderings up and down the slopes of the hills that divided them from their old home, and here he often met a solitary monk returning to his lonely cell after visiting his afflicted brethren in the city. Sometimes the news thus obtained was more cheering. The prison doors had been opened for one or two, and they had been allowed to depart, and then Arethusa would talk of

returning to their city home, that John might re-
sume his studies under Libanus; but before any
definite arrangements could be made for this a
message of warning would come from the bishop
or some friend begging them to stay a little longer
in safety, and this was generally accompanied by
a story of cruel mutilation or violent death, and
that Julian was fast becoming a fierce persecutor.
A little later and the wonder at this was lost in the
startling intelligence that the emperor had undertaken to restore the Temple at Jerusalem, and had
sent an army of workmen to clear away the ruins
and rubbish from the ancient site.

Placidia turned pale when John came in one day
and brought this news, but his mother only smiled
at what she considered as his mistake. "It is folly
to suppose Julian would do such a thing as that,"
she said; "who could have told thee such a foolish
tale, my son?"

"Nay, but it is not a foolish tale, mother. The
Jews are even now preparing for a grand festival
in honor of the emperor, and there will be great
rejoicings. Several monks told me this."

Arethusa glanced at Placidia. "Can it be that
the prophecy of the old Jewish slave-dealer is to be
verified?" she whispered.

But John, with a boy's eagerness to tell all the
news, would not wait for Placidia to speak. "The
Christians will soon be entirely crushed, they say,
for they are not to be allowed to hold any public

office, and heavy taxes will be imposed upon them to support the pagan temples."

"Nay, nay, my son; it cannot be so bad as that," said the widow hopefully, and noticing how deeply affected Placidia looked.

John noticed her altered looks, too, and said quickly, "What is it, my Placidia; art thou ill?"

"No, not ill; but this news about the Jewish temple, art thou quite sure it is true?"

"Yes, I could not be mistaken, for I saw a number of Jews set off on their journey southward while I was talking to a monk near the city gates."

His mother looked up quickly. "Thou must not venture too near the city, my son," she said in an anxious tone. It was chiefly on his account that she was still staying at Daphne, for she feared some-one besides herself might have heard his incautious speech about the shrine being miraculously destroyed, and if it were reported to the emperor John would inevitably be seized and thrown into prison.

Placidia, who knew how anxious Arethusa was about this, now proposed that they should leave Daphne and journey southward too. Melissa was anxious to reach Alexandria, for news had come that their beloved bishop, Athanasius, had once more been restored to his flock, and so a time of peace might confidently be expected in the city as well as in the Church, for he was greatly beloved by all classes. So Placidia persuaded Arethusa that

a journey as far as Jerusalem would be very agreeable just now, even if they did not go all the way to
Egypt.

John was, of course, delighted at the plan, until
he suddenly remembered that Placidia might wish
to stay in her native city.

"Nay, if I went to Alexandria I should not stay,
for there are none there now who would care to
see Placidia, while here—"

"We could not spare thee from Antioch long,"
interrupted John, "for thou art the best nurse to
the sick and the best comforter to the sorrowful.
I have heard it again and again from the deacons
that no one is so welcome among the poor as Placidia, my mother's friend. Did any ever know thou
wert a slave?" he asked in a subdued tone.

"Yes, it is no secret among our friends," answered Placidia; "but it was not mentioned to thee
until lately, because thy mother set me at liberty at
the time of her marriage, when she received me
from her father, and it was painful to her to hear
me speak of my captivity."

"And thou wert a lady, a nun, and a slave," said
John musingly.

"Yes, but above all a Christian," said Placidia;
"and to serve the Lord Christ by any means hath
been the aim of my life."

"And—and thou couldst serve the Lord better as
a slave than as a nun?" asked John.

"Yes, better in the world than in the desert," said

Placidia decidedly. "It may seem strange, too, but I have lived nearer the Lord, enjoyed closer and sweeter communion with him, since I have been busy helping others than when I shut myself up in the tower at home and vainly thought to shut the world out."

"Was it in vain, then?" asked the lad.

"Yes, for I took my world with me—my pride—for I was very proud in those days. What is thy world, John?" she asked with a grave smile.

The boy shook his head. "Whatever it is, thou wouldst say I shall take it with me to the monastery and have to fight against it there," he said.

"Fight or yield," said Placidia, "putting on a monk's dress doth not ensure us the victory, or we should not have so many proud, arrogant, ignorant monks as the Church is now troubled with."

"And thou thinkest it is better—nobler—to fight against our world—our besetting sins—while doing ordinary everyday work," said John thoughtfully.

"Yes, I do; and thou knowest what thy mother thinketh about it, John Chrysostom." Placidia always used his surname if she wished to be particularly impressive.

"Yes," answered John, "I have feared sometimes that my mother would break her heart if I became a monk," and he stooped and dipped his fingers in the marble basin of the fountain near which he was sitting.

The widow had left the inner court, where they were sitting, to talk to Melissa about the proposed

BESETTING: *constantly troubling*

journey, so that he could talk freely to Placidia upon this topic, which lately had become an all-absorbing one in his thoughts. "I am afraid it would almost kill my mother," he went on, "and yet I do not see why it should."

"Ah, thou knowest nothing of the great love she hath for thee," said Placidia. "Thou dost forget that thou art her only child, and that for thy sake—to watch over thee and give thee the best education in her power—she hath voluntarily lived a life of widowhood ever since she was twenty—she was not twenty when thy father, Secundus, died and left thee an infant to her care. He was a noble soldier, John, but not so noble as thy mother."

"Nobody could be as noble as she, thou knowest," rejoined the boy warmly. "I heard my teacher speak of her one day, and he said, 'What wives these Christians have!'"

"Yes, she is the noblest woman in Antioch," said Placidia.

"And to break her heart would be wicked indeed. Placidia, thou shalt tell her that I will not ask again to be a monk; I will go on with my study of the law, be the best lawyer in Antioch, perhaps, if she lives; but—but if she should die I think I must fly from the world."

The conversation was here interrupted by the return of Arethusa with Melissa. She was, of course, delighted at the thought of setting out on her journey homeward, for she had begun to grow weary of Antioch before the emperor came, and now she was still more impatient to hasten her departure.

So after several plans had been discussed, it was at length decided that Arethusa should pay a visit to the city, to arrange with a family of Jews whom she had befriended to travel with them and make all the needful changes in her household. John and Placidia would both have accompanied her, but she would not hear of it. There was less danger for her to travel alone, she said, and so after walking with her for a short distance they returned to the village, and the widow went on in her litter alone.

As soon as the city gates were reached, the news was confirmed that Julian, to vex the Christians, had professed himself the friend and patron of the Jews, and to prove the worthlessness of the prophecy which foretold their continued dispersion and the prostration of their temple and worship, undertook to restore them to their own land and rebuild the temple. Numerous other edicts were talked of as having been issued, but all of the same tendency—to put down the Christian religion at all costs and elevate paganism to its old position. But men laughed at the attempt to revive what had been worn out long before, and which scarcely needed the light of the Gospel to push it from its place.

So the struggle soon resolved itself into this— Christianity or no religion at all; for, of course, Judaism was for the Jews, and no one thought of it

PROSTRATION: *ruin*

as applicable to any other nation.

Meanwhile the Christians of Antioch gave themselves to prayer and fasting, humbling themselves before the Lord in their affliction, patiently submitting themselves to the new prefect and magistrates, paying the taxes imposed, and bearing as meekly as they could the gibes and jeers of the triumphant Jews, for whom everything went on merrily just now. Paganism was dead, they knew, and nothing could revive its corpse, and the death-blow had been struck at this hateful Christianity, and their glorious temple was to be rebuilt at Jerusalem. What was to prevent them regaining their old power, and having seated one of the royal race of David on the ancient throne, make the rest of the nations tributary—even Julian himself would be little better than an emperor in name only when that glorious day should dawn.

This was the dream of many a busy, plotting Jewish brain in Antioch as they gathered their wealth of gold, silver, and slaves and prepared for their emigration. In the poorer quarter of the town their brethren were not less busy, for giving up the practice of magic and fortune-telling, buying and selling small wares that yielded a large profit, they packed up what they could not convert into money and took their way to the ruined city of their forefathers—not now to weep over its desolation, but with songs of rejoicing to raise again the ancient walls and build its stately streets, and look forward to the time when the noise of boys and girls at play

GIBES: *taunts*

NATIONS TRIBUTARY: *nations that pay tribute*

there should cheer the hearts of its inhabitants. To labor at clearing away the rubbish of the ruins was not felt as a hardship by these peddling, huckstering Jews, unaccustomed as they were to manual toil of any kind, for love lightened their labor, and the hope of seeing Jerusalem the joy and wonder of the whole earth made every hardship of small account.

To build again the temple itself was the special aim of Julian, for in doing this he knew he should strike a blow at Christianity that would be keenly felt, even if it were not absolutely fatal to its continuance, for it had been prophesied that the temple should remain desolate and the Jews dispersed, and to prove this false was the great aim of the apostate, for he had little love for the Jews themselves. So a large number of skilled workmen had been engaged to clear the spot where the sacred building once stood, that wonder of the world that all the care and energy of the conquering Titus failed to save from such utter destruction that not one stone was left upon another, and it was not certainly known just where it was situated.

When these imperial laborers arrived from Cæsarea they were met with songs of welcome from the assembled Jews, and they may have thought that here they were secure from the greed and rapacity of the money-loving people; but if so they were mistaken, for such a good opportunity of driving bargains was not to be lost, and the peddling and money-lending, fortune-telling, and slave-dealing

HUCKSTERING: *haggling*
RAPACITY: *plundering*

went on as briskly round the sacred ruins as in the streets of Antioch or Constantinople.

Among those assembled here were some of the family of old Deborah, and now that her oft-repeated words seemed likely to be fulfilled, they spoke of her as a "wise woman," a prophetess, to whom it was an honor to belong; and with this came the recollection of an oath she had made them swear before she died, that when her prophecy should be fulfilled they should bring her body and lay it in the sacred earth of her native land.

They were discussing when and how this had better be done, and whether it would be possible to have her tomb within sight of the new temple, when their attention was attracted by signs of confusion on the distant mound of rubbish and ruined columns.

"Only some miserable Gentile quarrel," remarked one contemptuously.

"Nay, nay, it is more than that, for the men are leaving their work in hot haste and flying down the hill," said another, after gazing steadily toward the spot for several minutes.

His companions looked as though they doubted him, and rose from their seats inside the tent and came and stood near the entrance themselves. "Yes, they are leaving certainly," remarked one. "Can the emperor have been bought over by these Christians, thinkest thou?" he added, looking at his friends in perplexity; "if so, the Jews must outbid them—wealth is power—the only power we possess as yet; and we must use that to gain the rest—the throne of our fathers—and then—then—" the speaker spread his arms abroad and gazed across the valley to the city of ruins—"Jerusalem shall be the joy of the whole earth and the mistress of nations, and the God of Abraham, Isaac, and Jacob shall rule them with a rod of iron."

From these splendid dreams of his fallen country's greatness he was recalled by seeing a party of men running toward them.

"What is it? What hath happened?" asked several in a breath, stepping forward to meet them.

"Fire, fire!" shouted the newcomers.

"Where is it? we see no fire," replied the others, looking across toward the ruins.

"It is there; the men are flying from it," and they rushed on as though a fiery deluge were in swift pursuit.

"It is a Nazarene trick to prevent the temple from being rebuilt. I will go myself and see what hath caused all this confusion," said the Jew; and leaving the others in charge of the tent and the rich store of silk and other merchandise they had brought with them, he hastened down the slope toward the spot from which everyone was flying. In a short time, however, he returned, looking sadly perplexed and disturbed. "There is fire it is certain," he said. "I have seen it myself leaping up and licking round the ruins, but how it came there I know not."

"And thou didst not ask!" exclaimed one of his companions.

"Nay, I needed not to ask, for these Gentile dogs are crying that it came down from heaven."

"And thou dost believe them!"

"Am I a Nazarene—a follower of the carpenter's son?" asked he in bitter scorn. "Nay, nay, they may tell me what they please, but I say I know not whence it came, but that it shall speedily be extinguished I swear, and the emperor informed of this Nazarene trick to stop the work of building."

To extinguish the mysterious fire became the first thought of the Jews now, and they labored unremittingly—carrying water and pouring it over every mound of rubbish, and heaping earth and mud wherever a tiny flame appeared, and by this means the flames were at length subdued, and in a few days the workmen once more ventured to pick up their tools and recommence the work of clearing the fallen stones and rubbish from the sacred site—the Jews watching with jealous eyes lest another trick should be played upon them and the work hindered.

But in spite of their eager, anxious watching, the alarm was soon spread again that the fire had broken out afresh and with renewed vigor, some having fallen into the flames and been seriously burned this time. The Jews, however, were prepared for this, and by dint of great energy and care prevented the panic from spreading very far,

UNREMITTINGLY: *without ceasing*
BY DINT: *by means of*

so that only a few ran off in terror, and they were induced to return upon the promise of a liberal reward to assist in extinguishing the flames.

But it was all in vain. Extinguished in one place the flames broke out in another, leaping, dancing, licking over the stones, as if claiming them as their own, and holding them in a fiery embrace. Even the Jews began to quail now, but they would not let the panic-stricken workmen see it, but talked of Nazarene tricks still, and urged the men, by alternate threats of the emperor's displeasure and promises of their own gold, to commence work once more.

A few were induced to pick up their tools, and recommence the unequal contest, while the rest stood in anxious crowds to see the result of this before they ventured upon what seemed to them not only a dangerous, but an almost impious attempt to fight against God.

And truly it seemed as though God was fighting against this, for no sooner was a little of the debris removed than the flames leaped forth again, many in their excitement declaring they could see them descend from the sky before they leaped up from the earth. But whether from firedamp or some other unexplained cause, certain it was that the more the men dug the higher the flames leaped forth, until at length none would venture near the spot, and the undertaking had to be abandoned, for the present at least.

LIBERAL: *generous*
QUAIL: *lose heart and fear*
IMPIOUS: *disrespectful to God*

A bitter wail of disappointment was raised when the anxious Jews heard this decision, and many of them accused the Christians of practicing magic, saying that the fire had been caused by the intervention of Satan in their favor.

"It was well we did not bring the body of Deborah with us," said her kinsman as he sadly turned from the scene of desolation around which so many hopes clustered and had been crushed.

"Her prophecy is not likely to be fulfilled yet, Onias," said another, with a deep-drawn sigh.

"Thinkest thou the emperor will make another attempt?"

"I fear the Christians will outbid us. They are rich now, and not the despicable sect they were sixty years ago."

"True, they are rich, Onias," assented his friend.

"But Julian hateth them for helping to murder his relatives, and will crush them by any means."

"If—he—can," said the other slowly. "I have watched this movement, my Abdiel, and thou hast but to think of one man, and the changes and chances of his life, to know that the Church will not bow to the emperor always. Look at the patriarch of Alexandria, Athanasius. Three times hath he been banished for withstanding the edicts of one emperor or the other, and is at last recalled by Julian to be once more the idol of Alexandria."

"Then thou thinkest these Christians possess

FIREDAMP: *a flammable gas often found in coal mines*

so much power that Julian dare not renew the attempt?"

"Nay, I said not so; for I hope, as hundreds of our countrymen do, that we shall yet regain our ancient power by means of our enslaver—Rome. Yes, yes, we will hope for this," he said, rousing himself with sudden energy; "we must wait and watch and plot and scheme, and, above all things, gain wealth a little longer, only a little longer, and then the name of Nazarene shall be trampled out of the earth."

Very different was the scene in the next tent to that occupied by this party of Jews, for there our friends from Daphne sat silent, but with rejoicing hearts. John could hardly be restrained from singing aloud one of the Psalms of David when he knew that the attempt to rebuild the temple had so signally failed.

"Placidia, I must say it if I cannot sing it," he said at last, and with a glowing face and flashing eyes he repeated the first part of the ninety-eighth Psalm: "O sing unto the Lord a new song; for he hath done marvelous things: his right hand, and his holy arm, hath gotten him the victory. The Lord hath made known his salvation: his righteousness hath he openly showed in the sight of the heathen."[1]

"I am not afraid of old Deborah's prophecy now," whispered Placidia, turning to Arethusa; "the spell is broken at last, and I *know* that Christianity will triumph."

[1] PSALM 98:1-2
SIGNALLY: *notably*

Chapter XVI

Monica and Her Son

THE first rays of the rising sun were glancing through the topmost boughs of an ancient and stately grove, that formed a leafy screen around Tagaste's temple of Isis, and closed it in from the din and bustle of the town. The white marble of the temple could as yet be seen but dimly in the early light, but the sacred Ibis had been aroused from her nest and was now stalking up and down in front of the altar, around which flamen and sacrificing priests were already busy. On a pedestal in the interior building stood Isis and the mystic Horus, but they were not the only Egyptian deities that graced the shrine. The dog-headed Anubis, and the ox Apis, besides more uncouth idols, were here in silent, solemn majesty; while beyond the rail that divided the worshipers from the officiating priests stood an eager company of merchants, who had come to consult the goddess of commerce and agriculture upon their plans, and to learn, if possible, what success would attend their different ventures.

FLAMEN: *priests*
UNCOUTH: *strange, foreign*

One of those most eager to reach the dividing-rail was Patricius Augustinus, a citizen of Tagaste, who led by the hand his only son, Aurelius, a boy about ten years old, who was more occupied with watching the movements of the priests, and occasionally treading on the bystanders' toes, than with any thought about the sacredness of the place or the present solemnities.

It was about this boy that Patricius desired to consult the goddess, for he was quick and clever, and gave promise of being an eminent lawyer, or rhetorician, if his father could only provide the means of giving him a good education, and—one other "if"—he could make up his mind to overcome his idle, mischievous habits.

Augustine—for by this name he is most generally known—was not a good boy, and he knew that this visit to the temple of Isis would deeply grieve his mother; for although his father was a heathen and worshiper of the old gods of Egypt, Monica was a devout and earnest Christian, and sorely grieved at the waywardness of her son as well as the passionate obstinacy of her husband. Whatever the oracle of Isis might give in the way of encouragement to other worshipers, Patricius was pleased with the answer he obtained this morning.

"The son of Tagaste will live in the memory of nations yet unborn," pronounced the seer, who happened to know young Augustine, and doubtless thought if his augury did not suit this boy it

AUGURY: *prophecy*

would some other at all events; and so, after the
sacrifice had been offered, the incense burned,
and the customary rite completed, Patricius and
his son returned home in time to meet Monica as
she came from church.

"Where hast thou been so early, my Patricius?"
asked the lady timidly as she took Augustine's
hand and looked anxiously down at his merry but
determined face.

"I have been to the temple of Isis," said the boy
before his father could reply; "and—and what did
the oracle say, my father?" he asked, turning to
Patricius.

"Not that thou wouldst be a Christian. So thou
mayest as well give up thy prayers, Monica, and let
the boy have his own way," he said, speaking to his
wife in no very pleasant tone.

The lady did not reply for fear these angry words
should be followed by blows, but silently shook her
head and clasped the little hand she held tighter
within her own as they silently walked through the
busy streets of Tagaste to their home.

It seemed that Monica was to be more than usually tried this morning, for her husband's mother,
who lived with them, and who hated her because
of her strong attachment to Christianity, met her
with bitter reproaches about various little domestic matters, the cause of which was explained a
little later when a friend called to ask if she were
ready to accompany her to the house of another

friend, to whom Monica was strongly attached. "I did not know thou wert going," said Monica in a little surprise.

"Nay, but Alypus, her husband, came this morning to tell thee of their sore trouble, and ask if thou wouldst go to them, and take Augustine with thee, to spend a few hours at least."

"Then it was while I was at church, and my mother saw him," rejoined Monica quickly. "Is our Parthenia sick again?" she added.

"Nay, it is ill tidings concerning the mother of Alypus that hath just reached them; and as thou hast heard Parthenia was not very kind to her in Alexandria, she blames herself as the cause of her going on this pilgrimage to Jerusalem, instead of following her son to Tagaste, as everyone thought she would."

"My Parthenia may be to blame—she herself says she was very blameworthy, but it may be her mother was not less so," and Monica sighed as she thought how her life was often embittered, and how hard it was to please her husband's mother sometimes. She scarcely knew whether she ought to leave home now, even for a few hours, as the old lady was so cross; but again thinking of her friend's trouble she resolved to go to her chamber and consult with her, and so, while her friend rested in the inner court, she went to see her.

She returned in a short time bringing Augustine with her, for he had long been promised this visit to his young friend Adeodatus.

"Now, tell me all the tidings Alypus brought this morning," said Monica when they had left the house and were fairly on their way. "Who brought the news concerning his mother," she asked.

"One of the slaves who went with her on this pilgrimage. She was obliged to sell her at Damascus she says, for Melissa was taken ill while on her way to Antioch."

"To Antioch!" repeated Monica; "but wherefore did she wish to go to Antioch?"

"To meet her brother, who is one of the emperor's guards—a guard of the sacred labarum but that, as thou knowest, hath been laid aside by Julian."

Monica sighed. "These are evil times," she said, glancing at her boy as she spoke. "Did Melissa reach Antioch?"

"Nay, Alypus knows nothing concerning his mother but the tidings this slave hath brought, and she left her ill in the hospital at Damascus, and Parthenia is grieving sorely, and saying she hath caused her death."

On reaching the house of Alypus Augustine went in search of Adeodatus, who was in the garden, and here the two boys talked over the visit to the temple of Isis, and Augustine recounted his father's ambitious hopes on his account.

"And thou art to be a learned, eloquent man," said Adeodatus thoughtfully. "I wonder whether the oracle spoke truly."

"I know not—I do not believe in Isis or the

priests," said Augustine. "I wish I could!"

His companion looked surprised. "Thou dost wish to be a heathen!" he said.

"Yes, but I cannot; my father is, as thou knowest, and he is like the rest, he drinks wine and grows angry and cheats when he can, and—and—"

"Nay, thou wouldst not say thou dost wish to do the same," interrupted his friend.

Augustine blushed and looked confused. "I do and I do not," he said; "for I want to enjoy life—go to the theater and banquets, and drink wine, like my father, by and by; but—but—"

"What more wouldst thou say, Augustine?" asked his companion, looking greatly shocked.

"My mother will not let me. She does not know of these wishes, but she will not let me be happy now when I have done anything wrong, for she prays—Adeodatus, thou knowest not how hard she prays."

"And God will answer her prayer, Augustine. Imogene, our nurse, hath talked to us a great deal about this. I wish thou couldst hear her some-times."

"And I wish thou couldst hear my mother sometimes," said Augustine, "she almost makes me want to be a Christian, only I want to be angry, too, when my father and grandmother are so cross and scold her. Her God is the true God, I know, and I mean to love and serve Him by and by, as my mother does, but I must enjoy the world a little first. I have prayed about this

—asked the Lord Christ to change my heart by
and by, but I do not want to be a Christian just
yet."

"But, Augustine, suppose there should be no by
and by—suppose the plague should come again, as
it did last year, and thou shouldst be stricken with
death," said Adeodatus solemnly.

Augustine shuddered and turned pale for a moment, but he soon shook off this momentary fear
and said, "O, never mind the plague! let us play
under this apple-tree and forget such dull things.
These apples are ripe," he said, looking up at the
tempting fruit.

"My father does not think they are quite ripe
enough to be plucked," said Adeodatus, glancing
upward, and then he proposed that they should
go to an arbor at a little distance.

But Augustine looked longingly up at the
branches. "I like apples," he said wistfully.

"We shall have some when Imogene comes,"
said Adeodatus, moving away from the tree as
he spoke, while, at the same moment, Augustine
picked up a stone and threw it among the branches. It came down again at his feet, and with it, rus-
tling through the leaves, came an apple as well. He
picked it up and ran after his companion, but hid
the apple in the folds of his loose robe until they
had reached the arbor.

Adeodatus stared when he took it out. "I do
not think my father would like us to pluck those
apples."

"He need not be troubled," said Augustine cool-
ly. "Thou canst have a few apples, I should think,
without telling him. Thou shalt have this and I
will go and fetch another," and before Adeodatus
could speak he had run back to the tree, and another apple came falling through the branches to
the ground.

"We must make haste and eat them," said Adeodatus.

Augustine began to eat it at once, but he did not
enjoy the taste of the rich, ripe fruit, it was quite
evident, and his companion was not greatly surprised to see him throw more than half of it over
the wall. His own soon followed, and then the two
boys sat and looked at each other for a minute or
two without speaking.

"What art thou thinking of?" asked Augustine,
at last trying to throw off the miserable feeling
that oppressed him.

For answer Adeodatus burst into tears. "I can
never be a monk now," he said, "and I can never
talk to Imogene about it again. O, Augustine! we
have been stealing, and Imogene will be so sorry
when I tell her."

"But thou art not obliged to tell her," said Augustine, stoutly trying to overcome his own disposition to cry. The effort, however, was a failure,
and the next minute he sobbed out, "O, mother,
my mother, I have sinned again; I cannot keep
from sinning continually, and I cannot be happy
in my sin."

DISPOSITION: *inclination*

"Thank God, then, my son," said a voice at his elbow, and looking up, Augustine saw Imogene, the nurse, of whom his companion had spoken.

She was a slave and not very young, and evidently a foreigner, from her fair complexion and the peculiar accent with which she spoke the Greek tongue.

Augustine started and looked confused when he saw her gazing at him with her clear, searching blue eyes, but she only laid her hand tenderly on his head and said in a gentle voice, "Thou art Aurelius Augustinus, the son of Monica."

"Dost thou know my mother?" asked Augustine.

"Nay, but I have heard of her as a pattern to all wives and mothers in Tagaste, and thou wilt thank God some day that Monica was thy mother."

Glancing at her own charge, she saw that he looked disturbed and uncomfortable as well as Augustine. "What hath happened, my Adeodatus? Thou art unhappy, I can see," and she sat down and drew the child toward her.

But Adeodatus resisted the caress. "I am not worthy, Imogene," he sobbed. "I have soiled my baptismal robes with sin this day, and can never become a holy monk."

"And is it the first time, thinkest thou, that they have been soiled—thy white garments of baptism?" asked Imogene tenderly.

Adeodatus looked surprised. "I have been guilty of a great sin," he sobbed.

"Not greater than Christ's blood can wash away," replied Imogene. "Thou hast never felt that thou hadst committed sin before, and therefore thou didst not know thy need of a Saviour; but now that thou knowest thy white garments are stained with sin thou wilt seek the only remedy, 'the blood of Jesus Christ, which cleanseth us from all sin.'"[1]

"But, Imogene, thou dost forget I have only just committed this sin; I have not done penance for it yet, and so—"

"The Lord Christ will forgive it at once," said Imogene quickly; "if thou dost confess thy sin to Him He will pardon before the penance is performed."

But Adeodatus still shivered with fear. "If I were a holy monk and had only forgotten some rule, or eaten something I ought not, the Lord Christ might forgive me; but this is a real sin."

"And the Lord Christ died for real sins, not imaginary ones," said Imogene, who had no great love for monks or nuns either.

But Adeodatus still shrank from telling her what he had done, for he thought he should forfeit her good opinion, perhaps her very love, and the little neglected boy, who was rarely noticed by his mother, loved Imogene very much. At length he whispered, "Tell me about the thief on the cross and the virgin-mother standing by."

Imogene told him the story of the crucifixion, but she was careful to add that it was the Saviour

---

[1] I JOHN 1:7

"THE LORD CHRIST DIED FOR REAL SINS"

Himself, without any pleading look from His mother, who had compassion on the thief.

"I am a thief, too," whispered Adeodatus. "We took some apples off the tree. May we go to the Lord Jesus with such a sin as that?"

"To whom couldst thou go but to Him? He is the Saviour, and—"

"Yes, but He is so great and high and holy, so—so far off from us," whispered the boy through his tears. "That is why my mother hath a statue of the virgin in her chamber, for being a woman she can feel for us, and it is easier to go to her."

Imogene looked troubled as she stroked the boy's hair tenderly. "I learned to love the Lord Christ from the lips of one whose father had died for the faith in the great persecution, but she said naught concerning the Lord's mother beyond this, that she was a good and holy woman. She did not pray to her, and was not afraid of taking her troubles and sorrows to the Lord, for she taught me that He could be touched with the feeling of our infirmities, that He had taken our whole nature upon Him, and knew the love of a mother's heart, and had promised to give us that love. I have heard this, too, from the Scriptures. 'As one whom his mother comforteth,'[1] are God's words, and so there can be no need to ask the intercession of Mary when Christ can feel for us Himself."

Augustine sat and listened to every word. "Thou dost talk like my mother," he said as she

---

[1] Isaiah 66:13

concluded. "She told me that it was a mistake to think the Lord was so holy that He could not feel for sinners even in their sin, and it is thinking of this that makes me so miserable sometimes. I seem to see the Lord Christ looking as pitiful and sorrowful as my mother does when I have been doing wrong. He is like my mother, I think," added the boy.

"Monica is like Christ in her gentleness and love for thee, my son, only, if it be possible, He is more pitiful, more tender than even thy mother, and deeply as she may grieve over thy sins His grief is greater, because He is holier and He loves thee so much more."

The conversation was interrupted here by Alypus calling the boys from the covered terrace which united the garden to the house, and so, hastily removing all traces of their sorrow, they ran toward him, leaving Imogene in the arbor to ponder over what had happened.

PITIFUL: *compassionate*

Chapter XVII

The Letter

MONICA sat with her friends in the *triclinium* talking over the news of the Church
in Tagaste, and how great cause for thankfulness
they had in their freedom from persecution, since
the news had come of the cruel edicts issued by Julian against the Christians of Antioch. Then Alypus entered leading the two boys, whom he placed
beside Monica; at the same time ordering a slave
to bring a fresh basket of fruit for them. But Adeodatus shook his head when the grapes and apples
were handed to him, and instead of eating them
burst into tears. Augustine likewise looked confused and uncomfortable, but helped himself to
a bountiful supply, which he ate while his mother
tried to comfort his companion.

When he had finished and Adeodatus had left
off crying, Monica whispered a command to her
son which evidently did not please him, for he
pouted and shook his shoulders. "I do not like
Homer," he muttered; "I hate the Greek tongue.
Let me recite one of the plays of our own Egyptian

TRICLINIUM: *dining room*
HOMER: *a Greek poet; writer of the Iliad and the Odyssey*

Terence, or some of the poetry of Virgil."

"Let it be something from our comic Terence," said Alypus, who had overheard these words; and Augustine, looking well-pleased at this opportunity of exhibiting his youthful powers, stood up between the three tables that formed the dining-room suite, and, facing Parthenia, commenced his dramatic recital.

Monica looked as pleased as Augustine himself when she saw that by his impassioned tone, flashing eyes, and the quick nervous movement of his hands the whole attention of her friends was riveted upon him, and her heart glowed proudly as she thought of his probable future, when he became—as she hoped he would—the most learned and eloquent rhetorician of Carthage.

It would not do, however, to let Augustine see she was so pleased, for he was already too fond of this light poetry, but very idle over the more solid part of his education. So when Alypus had applauded him on the conclusion of the piece and had handed him another bunch of grapes as a reward, she said quietly, "It costs but little labor to learn Terence. I wish our Euclid had as great charm for my Augustine."

"Nay, not like our great mathematician, Euclid!" exclaimed Alypus in well-feigned surprise. "Nay, nay, it cannot be but that Augustine is fond and proud of his fellow-countryman. He is a true Egyptian, I am sure."

"Yes, I am glad Euclid was an Egyptian as well as

TERENCE: *a Roman playwright*
VIRGIL: *a Roman poet; writer of the Æneid*

Terence—that the Romans are not masters every-where—but I do not like learning his elements of geometry."

Alypus shook his head and laughed. "Adeodatus will pass thee in that study if thou art not careful and industrious. He cares little for Terence or Virgil, but will sit patiently over a proposition of Euclid until it is mastered."

"I wish he would master mine for me, then," said Augustine impatiently. "I like playing at ball better than learning about circles and angles."

Monica and Alypus both laughed, but quickly forgot the speech, for they recommenced the conversation about Melissa, and the disastrous news that had just arrived concerning the persecution at Antioch, so that the boys were quite forgotten for some time.

The sun had set, and little colored lamps had been hung between the white marble pillars, which shed a soft radiance through the room, before anyone thought of either Augustine or his companion, and then a slave was sent in search of them, for Monica was anxious to return home.

After looking in vain through the house they were found at last in the garden, both shivering from the dew that had fallen as they sat upon the grass, but still talking earnestly, for Augustine had persuaded Adeodatus to help him solve several problems from the detested Euclid, that he might have more time to play at ball or checkers the next day.

EUCLID: *a Greek mathematician; the "Father of Geometry"*
WELL-FEIGNED: *well-pretended*

Adeodatus was sent to Imogene in disgrace, and Monica scolded Augustine for staying out in the heavy night dew so late; but she was too anxious to reach home now to bestow much thought upon the danger he had thus incurred, and the circumstance was almost forgotten before he went to bed.

The next day, however, he was very unwell. Then Monica remembered the exposure to the heavy night dew, and treated him as for a cold or chill; but the sickness would not yield to her remedies, and at last he grew so much worse that she determined to have him baptized without delay. Augustine himself, however, was very unwilling for the rite to be performed. His mind dwelt upon Adeodatus, and his sorrow about the theft of the apple, which was not so much for the actual sin as that it had been committed after he was baptized, and, therefore, he had soiled his baptismal robes and incurred the greater guilt, and Augustine loved sin too well to be willing to give it up yet if he should be spared to get well again. He confessed his theft of the apple now to his mother, and begged her to pray that he might be forgiven by God; but at the same time he asked her not to send for the bishop to baptize him.

"If I get well again I—I shall sin again, perhaps; and then how dreadful it will be. Why was Adeodatus baptized so early, my mother?"

"His father wished it—wished him to be a child of

INCURRED: *brought upon himself*

God from his youth," said Monica, and she sighed
as she thought how earnestly she had prayed that
her son might give his life to God's service, and
yet how unwilling he was to be baptized because
it would be a check upon him in his sin. "I wish
thou hadst been baptized as Adeodatus hath; his
father told me how watchful and prayerful he is
lest he should defile his baptismal robes, and that
he himself was saved from many evil ways when
a young man by remembering the gentle, loving
teaching of his grandmother, and the words she
spoke to him when he was baptized—never to forget that his grandfather was a martyr."

"I wish my grandmother was gentle and kind
instead of being cross and finding fault with thee,
my mother," said Augustine, cleverly evading the
main point of which she had been speaking.

Unfortunately, the old lady had just entered
the chamber in time to hear these words, and she
turned toward Monica directly. "Thou dost teach
the boy to hate me," she said, "that thou mayest
make him a Christian the more easily."

"Nay, nay," said Monica, feeling confused and
vexed. "I have not said a word—"

"My mother would fain make me believe thou
art gentle and kind, but I know thou art not," interrupted Augustine hotly.

"Hush, hush, my son," said Monica, laying her
hand on his throbbing temples and compelling
him to be still; "thou wilt be worse if thou dost

grow angry. Do not speak to him, my mother," she said imploringly as she turned toward the old lady.

With a muttered exclamation she left the room, resolving to tell Patricius of this fresh insult as soon as he should return home, for she chose to believe still that Monica had tried to set the boy against her.

Fearing lest his mother in her anxiety for his conversion should even now send for the bishop to baptize him, Augustine begged his father's intervention in this matter, and Patricius, who cared for nothing but his son's advancement, readily promised that he should not be baptized until he wished it; for if Julian, their present emperor, still continued to hate Christianity, it was not likely to benefit his own son much. This was how he argued the matter to himself; but he persuaded Monica that it would be dangerous to excite the boy by the performance of this rite just at present, and his illness taking a favorable turn soon afterward, Monica gave up the hope once more, but continued to pray more earnestly than ever, not only for the conversion of her son, but for her husband and his mother likewise.

Unconsciously to herself, perhaps, her hopes for her boy were much more sanguine than for Patricius, and she began to look for some fruit of her labor—some answer to her prayers for him; and yet it was to Patricius and his mother that the de-

SANGUINE: *confident*

sired blessing came first, for it was about this time that her husband first began to leave off attending the feasts and drunken revels held in honor of the old gods, and even showed some little kindness and consideration for Monica, which he had never done before since their marriage.

The first instance of this change—this lately awakened interest in her and her Christian friends—greatly surprised Monica, for Patricius brought home the news that he had just heard from a party of Jews, who had come from Jerusalem, that one of their number had been entrusted with a letter by a Christian lady to her son Alypus, a merchant of Tagaste.

"They came to me to inquire where they might find Alypus," explained Patricius; "for they had searched through the town in vain, until one suggested asking one of the town officers, who would be sure to know."

"It was well they came to thee. Is the letter delivered to Alypus yet, thinkest thou?" asked Monica.

"Thou shouldst go and ask if these Jews have been to him."

His mother looked up, and would have raised some objection, but for once her son would not hear a word against his wife. "Monica hath been in close attendance upon Augustine during his illness, and her own health will suffer if she keeps so closely within the house," he said.

So Monica set off once more to inquire about

the truth of this strange rumor of a letter coming from Melissa—whether it was true, or only a Jewish trick to obtain a liberal reward by producing a fictitious letter written by someone else.

She found Alypus in a state of great excitement and uncertainty as to what he should believe and what he should do, for the letter brought by these Jews was not written by his mother—it was not in her handwriting—but purported to come from his Aunt Placidia, whom he scarcely remembered to have heard of beyond this, that she had mysteriously disappeared from Alexandria. He knew it was owing to this that his father had entertained a dislike and suspicion of the Jews as being the cause of his aunt's disappearance, and which made him the more suspicious of them now as he read the strange epistle.

"It is only a trick of these crafty peddlers," he said at last, rolling up the strip of papyrus and throwing it aside; "they have gained what they wanted—the paltry reward for bringing this to me—and that is all they cared for;" and he was turning away to walk off his vexation in the garden, when Monica said gently,

"May I see this letter?"

"Yes, indeed; but I fear thou wilt not be able to read it, for the writer seems to have used the stylus but little of late," and Alypus handed her the roll as he spoke.

But at the first glance Monica shook her head.

EPISTLE: *letter*

"This is in Greek," she said, "and I know but little of that tongue—Latin being the language of Tagaste. Is Greek the language of Alexandria?" she asked.

"Yes, Alexandria was a colony of Greece once," said Alypus carelessly, and he was again turning toward the garden when Monica's voice arrested him.

"Would these Jews address a letter in Greek to Alypus of Tagaste, where the Latin tongue is spoken, thinkest thou?" she asked.

Alypus took up the roll again and looked at it more carefully. "These Jews know so much, and are banded together so closely and so secretly, that it is hard to judge what they do not know. But I will read the letter to thee;" and he sat down and read aloud.

"Placidia, the servant of Jesus Christ, to Alypus, greeting: Melissa, my beloved sister and thy mother, whose absence thou hast doubtless mourned, hath tarried with me at Antioch, hoping there to meet Quadratus, my brother, who is a guard in the service of the emperor. But he came not with Julian, as we hoped, and, being driven by the persecution to seek refuge in Judea, we came hither under the protection of some Jews, proposing to travel into Egypt with them. But while tarrying at Jerusalem thy mother, Melissa, was taken with a grievous sickness, and now lies weak and helpless, strong only in her love to thee and her desire to see thee before the Lord removes her hence. If, therefore, this epistle be borne to thee faithfully by the Jews who have promised to take it, journey hither without delay, and I will tarry here until the calends of January. Delay not, therefore, thy coming, or send by a true messenger some word to thy mother and thy aunt,

PLACIDIA

"What thinkest thou, Monica?" he asked as he concluded his reading.

"That thy aunt hath truly sent it," said the lady decisively.

"But the latter part is what I do not like—this urging me to journey to Jerusalem. Thou dost not know these Jews; they have perhaps brought this from a band of robbers, who will lay wait for me in some of the valleys of Judea, and after robbing me demand a heavy ransom as the price of my liberty."

But Monica shook her head. "The Jews are bad enough, doubtless, but I do not think they are deceiving thee in this letter—it is a true letter."

"Then thou wouldst urge me to take this journey," said Alypus, glancing at his wife as he spoke.

Parthenia was lying on a couch indolently toying with her fan, but she started at the word "journey." "I cannot spare thee from home long, Alypus," she said. "Where dost thou purpose to go?"

CALENDS: *first days*

"My mother is at Jerusalem, and desires to see me," said her husband, trying to appear indifferent, although it was evident he was anxious to start on this journey since Monica advised it.

But at the mention of going to his mother Parthenia looked angry and hurt, and she said in a petulant tone, "She can come to us, Alypus, of course, but I cannot spare thee to go to her."

"Nay, nay; but, my Parthenia, think of the sorrow thou didst endure when thou wast in fear that Melissa might have died on this journey," interrupted Monica.

"But she is not dead," said Parthenia in the same petulant tone.

"But she is ill—very ill. Think, if it were thy Adeodatus, wouldst thou not be anxious to have him come to thee if thou wert sick and suffering?"

For answer Parthenia burst into tears, and Monica was left to comfort her alone, for Alypus was so vexed at his wife's unreasonable opposition to his taking this journey, that he went to walk in the garden and think over the matter more calmly, before finally deciding whether he would go himself or send a messenger instead.

While thinking over the strange circumstance of his aunt, whom he supposed to be dead, writing this letter to him, he suddenly remembered that Adeodatus had told him some story of Imogene meeting with a slave, who had said she was a lady of Alexandria. He had not paid much attention to

PETULANT: *irritable*

it at the time, but it recurred to his memory now, and he sent for Imogene to question her about it.

Having heard her account of her meeting with Placidia in the possession of some Jews, and parting with her afterward at Jerusalem, he asked if she thought she would recognize this lady-slave if she saw her.

"I am sure I should," answered Imogene confidently. "She hath grown old as well as the poor British captive, but I should know her anywhere."

"Then thou shalt go to Jerusalem, Imogene, and see the writer of this letter I have received. Thou art a discreet woman, and wilt obey my command in all things, I know; and as my business in Tagaste will be sorely hindered if I go myself, I will entrust the mission to thee."

The resolution had been so suddenly formed that Alypus forgot all the difficulties of a woman undertaking such a mission alone; but Imogene was not one to flinch from a duty because it was difficult, and the remotest hope of seeing Placidia once more was sufficient to lighten any toil, or strengthen her to brave any danger, so, with a smile of acquiescence, she said, "I will prepare with all speed, most noble Alypus, and thou wilt make all the arrangements needful," and she went back to her usual occupation, leaving the merchant with a heart greatly lightened by her willingness to go.

ACQUIESCENCE: *silent agreement*

Chapter XVIII

Suspense

SPRING flowers were blossoming in the gardens of Tagaste, and Epiphany hymns were being sung in the churches, telling of the manifestation of the Son of God to the sons of men, for the saturnalia had not yet been changed into Christmas, and so the glad songs with which we in these later ages hail this festive season were the Epiphany hymns of the early Church.

Alypus was expecting Imogene to return almost daily now, bringing with her his mother and his aunt, but as yet no tidings had come from the travelers, and he was growing anxious at the delay. Monica was their frequent guest, and Alypus trusted that through her example and persuasion Parthenia might accommodate herself to his mother more than she had done in Alexandria, for, of course, she would come to live with them again, and he hoped the household might go on more happily than before.

He was thinking of this matter one day while

SATURNALIA: *a week-long feast in honor of the Roman god Saturn, where slaves were free to do as they pleased*

on his way to the marketplace to meet with some other merchants, when, to his surprise, as he was passing the baths in the principal street he heard someone say, "There is Alypus, of Alexandria, my friend, so thou wilt not have to search for him far."

Pausing and looking round as he heard these words, Alypus saw an elderly, careworn, weather-beaten man, evidently a stranger in the town, who descended the marble steps of the building and hastened toward him at once.

After the usual salutation the stranger said, "I recognize thee now, Alypus, from thy likeness to thy mother."

"My mother!" repeated the merchant quickly. "Dost thou bring me tidings of my mother?"

"Nay, but I have come from Constantinople to see her. Is she not here in Tagaste?"

Alypus shook his head in bewilderment. "My mother came not hither with me when I left Alexandria," he said.

"But thou hast dwelt here some years—since Athanasius was expelled for George, of Cappadocia, to become patriarch, at the order of our late emperor, Constantius."

The merchant looked astonished. "Thou at least art acquainted with all my movements," he said. "Dost thou know Athanasius?"

"I was brought up with him in my youth," replied the stranger smiling, "and led thee to thy baptism."

VICISSITUDE: *variation*
PANDEMONIUM: *scene of chaos*

"Then thou didst know my grandmother," said Alypus quickly.

"Yes, she was my mother. Didst thou never hear of Quadratus, the guard of the labarum?" asked the stranger

For answer the merchant threw himself into his arms with an exclamation of joyful surprise. "Quadratus," he repeated, "I have heard my mother talk of thee many times, but we feared thou must have died, since we heard naught concerning thee for so many years."

The soldier shook his head with a grave, sad smile. "The life of our noble patriarch, Athanasius, hath scarcely been of greater vicissitude than mine. I have been degraded, banished, recalled and honored, imprisoned and liberated, then honored again with the charge of the sacred standard of the cross, until Julian assumed the purple, and removed the name of Christ, as well as the cross, from its rightful place, and then I retired from the service of arms, and as soon as my affairs in Constantinople could be arranged I set off to Alexandria."

"And thou didst find it a pandemonium under this patriarch, George," interrupted Alypus.

"Nay, the city was quiet and orderly, for it had wreaked a terrible vengeance on this cruel oppressor, who had usurped the seat of God's servant. Hast thou not heard that this George was dragged through the streets like a malefactor and drowned?"

USURPED: *wrongfully taken*
MALEFACTOR: *criminal*

"Then thou didst not see the city under its Arian tyrant," said Alypus; "and thou, too, wilt call him a saint, as many are now doing, because he received a just reward for his evil deeds at the hands of those whom he cruelly oppressed." Alypus was angry.

"Nay, nay, be not so hasty in thy conclusions; doubtless, this murder of the patriarch was not an unprovoked deed, and I am not one to call him a saint on account of it, but many in Alexandria do, and, doubtless, he will be remembered as such, because of his violent and untimely end, when many a better man is forgotten."

Quadratus saw that his nephew could not speak with patience of the man who had driven him to seek an asylum in this provincial town to save himself from ruin, and so he told him of the joy of the citizens at the installation of Athanasius again, and their sorrow and threatened rebellion when banished once more by the order of Julian.

"But he hath not left his flock entirely this time," said Quadratus as he concluded his recital; "he hath retired to his father's tomb, beyond the city gates, where friends can visit him in secret, and he can still order the affairs of the Church."

Alypus sighed. "These are evil times," he said, "and the enemies of God's Church are victorious on all sides. Hast thou heard of the persecution in Antioch?"

"Yes, the tidings of this reached Alexandria while I was there," answered Quadratus.

"My mother was in Antioch, and fled from thence to Jerusalem."

"Thy mother alone in Antioch?" repeated Quadratus in a tone of surprise.

"Nay, nay, not alone; I had a letter brought to me by some Jews, written by one calling herself my Aunt Placidia."

Quadratus started. "Placidia!" he repeated. "Nay, nay, it cannot be true. My sister, Placidia, still living? where is she now? where has she been all these long years?"

But Alypus could only shake his head. "I am even now expecting the messenger I sent to Jerusalem in answer to this letter; tarry with me until she returns, and it may be thou wilt see both thy sisters together."

Quadratus agreed to this, because if he were to leave Tagaste in search of them now he might miss them; but the time passed more slowly to him than to his nephew, for he had little to engage his attention beyond walking out along the road the travelers were expected to pass, or talking to Adeodatus and hearing his account of his young friend, Augustine. He saw the boy himself sometimes, and Monica, his mother; he likewise heard from Alypus that, but for this lady, no notice would have been taken of the letter brought by the Jews, which made him take more notice of both than he otherwise might have done. What he saw of young Augustine did not please him, and he shook his head gravely as he saw how often he cheated while playing some game with Adeodatus, and how idle he was while at his lessons. Talking with Monica one day he said, "Thy son is high-spirited and clever, but—"

"I know what thou wouldst say," interrupted Monica; "he is not a good boy—he is not a Christian. I know it, but I know that the grace of God can change the hardest heart, and this grace is given in answer to prayer, and will be given to my son even yet."

Quadratus looked at the earnest, loving face before him. "The kingdom of heaven suffereth violence, and the violent take it by force,"[1] he said thoughtfully.

She bowed her head. "I may well be violent in prayer for such a son, for he will be a great blessing or a great curse to the Church and to the world."

Quadratus turned his eyes upon the bright, eager-looking boy, now so ardently pursuing his play, and thought over Monica's words. As yet the appearances were all on the side of the curse coming upon many, but this might yet be averted through the simple prayer of faith, and the teaching from such a life as Monica's, who reminded him more of his own mother than anyone he had met before.

But with all the interchange of genial Christian

[1] MATTHEW 11:12

GENIAL: *pleasant*

converse with friends and the pleasant gossip of the baths, the days dragged on very slowly, waiting and watching for the messenger who did not come. They had heard about the attempt to rebuild the Temple, and of its utter failure, but this was all the news that came from Jerusalem, until at length Quadratus grew tired of waiting at Tagaste, and resolved to go to Alexandria again in search of his sisters, feeling sure that Melissa would decide to go there now that Athanasius had returned to the city.

This resolution of his uncle's decided Alypus to break off his connection with Tagaste and return to his native city, hoping that the change would restore his wife's health and spirits, for Parthenia had not been well for some time, which had been an additional reason against his taking the journey to Jerusalem, but which he half-regretted he had not done. Thus far no tidings had reached them of Imogene, and he feared now that, being a British woman, she had been seized by some Jewish slave-dealers and appropriated, for the Britons were lawful spoil as slaves in those times, whenever they could be taken and tamed. So he began to prepare for his removal to Alexandria, hoping to be able to effect this shortly after Easter, for the encyclical letter of Athanasius, issued at Epiphany, had fixed this later than usual this year. This duty devolved upon the pope or patriarch of Alexandria, because this city was the seat of all the

CONVERSE: *conversation*
ENCYCLICAL LETTER: *a letter to all the bishops*
DEVOLVED: *fell*

scientists, and possessed greater facilities for accuracy in studying the changes of the moon, which always determined the time for the observance of Easter. It was not known, therefore, with any certainty, until Epiphany, when Easter would be observed; but at that time notice was given, in all the churches of the world, of the date fixed by the patriarch of the great African Church, and no one thought of disputing it.

There would be little difficulty in removing from Tagaste so far as Imogene was concerned, for should her return be delayed beyond this time Monica and her husband would take charge of the travelers, and had promised to journey with them to Alexandria, for they were both anxious to visit the city that rivaled Carthage in its splendor and learning, as well to see the great Athanasius, who had so boldly stood forth as the champion of the Church against the oppression of its patron-masters—the successive emperors.

So the business concerns and household arrangements of Alypus were soon arranged for his departure from Tagaste, and preparations were commenced at once for the voyage to Alexandria, for they would travel by sea, and slaves were sent forward to engage a galley.

There was little danger in returning to Alexandria, for although Athanasius had again been banished, and was obliged to conceal himself in his father's tomb outside the city gates, the people were

so attached to him that Julian had not ventured to
appoint a successor to his chair; and though the
prefect was a devoted follower of Serapis, and had
restored the ancient service in the Serapeum, he
was too wise and politic a ruler to attempt laying
very heavy taxes upon the citizens, for they were
already restless enough, and riots had been all too
frequent of late for him to risk his power by provoking another.

There was little fear either that Julian would
visit Alexandria to stir up a persecution, for his
visit to Antioch had been anything but pleasant
to him, and he had left in disgust and retired to
Tarsus before the winter was over. He had started
for Persia now at the head of his army, determined
to subdue that ancient kingdom. Augurs and ora-
cles had prophesied perfect success to this expedition, and remembering the splendid victories
their emperor had gained in Gaul and Germany,
the soldiers forgot the previous reverses they had
suffered in Persia under Constantius, and departed from Tarsus full of joyful anticipations.

This was the latest news from the East that had
reached Alexandria, and the messenger bringing
these tidings reached the city just after Quadratus' return from Tagaste. He contrived to see the
courier, and question him about the state of affairs at Antioch, for he had sailed direct from the
mouth of the Orontes to the Egyptian metropolis,
and would, therefore, bring the news in a shorter

time than by a land journey through Syria. But although the news thus gained was recent and reliable, it was not very cheering.

Two hundred senators had been sent to prison in one day for daring to oppose some of Julian's plans; and, although they had been released soon afterward, the city was still smarting under the indignity thus offered to its noblest citizens, and the Christian Church was still suffering from his oppressive edicts, although the persecution had greatly abated in its fury since his departure, and some of those thrown into prison by his orders had since been released.

Quadratus questioned and cross-questioned the messenger, hoping to gain some tidings of his sisters; but the man had not heard anything of travelers returning from Jerusalem, excepting a few Jews, and so Quadratus resolved to await the coming of Alypus from Tagaste, and then set out himself in search of Placidia once more.

Chapter XIX

The Journey

MEANWHILE Imogene had reached Jerusalem after a toilsome, dangerous journey, for traveling in those days was not as easy as it is now, and was always attended with some peril from robbers infesting every mountain pass or lonely road, even if storms or contrary winds did not cause them great discomfort at sea.

Winds and robbers had both hindered Imogene, for the little galley in which she sailed had been driven about in the Mediterranean until her passengers and crew despaired of seeing land again, and only reached Cæsarea a mere wreck.

Imogene recognized the sailors' landmark—the temple of Sebasteum, perched on a rock in front of the town—long before they were able to enter the spacious harbor, for to the south and southwest immense blocks of stone, fifty feet long, had been sunk twenty fathoms, so that the only entrance was to the north; but once within the breakwater no storm could toss their little vessel, and so it was with thankful hearts and shouts of rejoicing from the sailors that the port was at last gained, and the marble palaces of the town came fully into view.

As soon as they had landed, however, Imogene started for Jerusalem, carefully concealing the money Alypus had given her to defray the expenses of her journey, and trusting that her appearance as an elderly slave would save her from any interruption from lurking robbers.

In this, however, she was disappointed, for soon after she had left Cæsarea a band of armed men came rushing out of one of the wild rocky ravines, and before Imogene could turn, or cry out for help, she was lifted by one of the men and carried off in his arms up the slope of the rocky defile as though she had been an infant instead of an old woman.

They seated her on a boulder of rock inside a cave, and then burst into a loud roar of laughter at her look of perplexity and distress as she began to implore them to release her. Her words would have had little effect even if they could have understood what she said; but they could not, neither could she comprehend a word spoken by them. Their actions, however, were all too easy of comprehension, for rough, rude hands were soon shaking her dress and searching every fold for concealed treasures, and it was not long before their accustomed fingers had found Imogene's hiding-place for her master's gold pieces, cunningly as it had been devised.

With a chuckling laugh the finder handed the

DEFRAY: *cover*
DEFILE: *narrow gorge*

little bag to his companions, and then went on to search for more. In vain Imogene begged, protested, and prayed them to return her money; the robbers only laughed at her tears and her strange language, and after satisfying themselves that they had taken all she possessed, they fastened her securely to the wall of the cave and then left her.

At first the poor woman was so overcome with grief and perplexity that she could think of nothing but her loss. As the hours stole on, however, and the shadows of evening darkened the cave, another fear succeeded this. Was she left here to die? Her answer to this came a few hours later, when one of the robbers returned, bringing some bread and a little sour wine.

Imogene had not seen this man before, but he seemed to be the interpreter of the band, for he spoke sufficient Greek to make her understand what he said, and asked several questions about the family she served, where they lived, whether they would be passing that road, and whether anyone at Cæsarea would ransom her.

All these questions Imogene answered truly; and, judging from her answers that little would be gained by detaining her any longer, the robbers set her at liberty the next morning.

Once more on her road to Jerusalem, Imogene traveled with all the speed she possibly could, for the calends of January had passed, and she feared Placidia might leave the city before she could reach it. Having been robbed of all her money, she had to depend for subsistence upon the charity of those she met on the road, to whom she repeated her tale of the robbery, which was, of course, an additional hindrance, and often delayed her some time.

Through all these adverse circumstances, January was almost at an end before the little colony that had gathered round the sacred Mount of Calvary was reached, and Imogene was travel-strained, weary, and footsore, as she walked down the street of Roman villas, to which she had been directed by Alypus.

To all her inquiries for Placidia, however, she received but one answer, a grave shake of the head, as a signal that she was not understood, and a finger pointed toward a large building at the further end of the town.

On drawing nearer to this she saw that it was a hospital, but she had a dim recollection of this having been the palace of the Empress Helena while she was living here. There were several monks and deacons on the steps as she drew near, and she ventured to ask one of these the question she had put to so many others in vain.

"Placidia?" repeated the deacon; "was she a visitor belonging to the Church of the Resurrection?"

"Nay, I know not; but that she came from Antioch during the late persecution," said Imogene anxiously.

"And thou hast come from Antioch in search of

her?" asked another of the deacons.

"Nay, I came from Tagaste, in Egypt. Canst thou tell me aught concerning her or her sister, Melissa, who was sick almost unto death here in Jerusalem?" said Imogene, in a voice of imploring earnestness.

"Thou sayest one was sick; was she an aged woman of Alexandria?" asked one.

"Yes; O, tell me, is she well? can I see her and Placidia?" and Imogene was so overcome that she burst into tears.

"Hush, hush, thou art weak and weary; enter and rest thyself, and one of the sisters will tell thee all concerning thy friends," and saying this the deacon led her into the hospital, and sent for one of the nurses.

"Bring a little wine and some bread to refresh this poor woman," said the deacon, "and then thou mayest tell her all thou knowest concerning Placidia and Arethusa of Antioch."

But Imogene shook her head when the wine was set before her. "Lead me to Placidia," she whispered. "I have hungered for her many weary years."

"Nay, but thou must eat and drink to gain strength, or else thou wilt never be fit to journey to Antioch," said the woman.

"To Antioch!" repeated Imogene; "hath my Placidia returned thither?"

"Yes, she tarried long in Jerusalem, waiting for a messenger to arrive from her sister's son; but no one came, and so when the calends of January were past she returned with Arethusa and John Chrysostom."

"And Melissa, her sister, is she—?" asked Imogene.

"She is better. I helped them to nurse her through her long and weary sickness, and traveled with her a short distance on her journey to Antioch."

"Then I, too, must go to Antioch," said Imogene with a weary sigh, and she would have risen at once to recommence her journey.

But the nurse gently laid her hand upon her shoulder, and compelled her to sit down again. "Thou must rest awhile and refresh thyself, for Antioch is many miles from here, and thou art worn and weary now;" and to take her attention from the present anxiety she began to tell Imogene of the recent attempt to rebuild the Jewish temple.

"The Jews were almost crazy with joy at the thought of this," she said; "and even delicate ladies came hither with silver spades to assist in removing the earth and rubbish from the sacred spot, while others carried it away in their mantles of embroidered silk."

"They must have been bitterly disappointed when the fire came," said Imogene as she thought of her long journey to Antioch, for she had no intention of returning to Tagaste until she had found Placidia.

"Yes, they were greatly disappointed—more even

MANTLES: *sleeveless cloaks*

than thou art now," said the nurse, who saw the direction of Imogene's thoughts; "but these things must be borne with patience, although they are often more trying than greater afflictions."

"Yes, I confess myself greatly disappointed that I cannot see Placidia," said Imogene with a sigh.

"Thou wilt see her soon; thou must stay here a few days for needful rest, and it may be some will come hither who are journeying to the great northern city, with whom thou mayest travel in safety."

This hope reconciled Imogene to the necessary delay, more than anything else, although her kind friend at the hospital took her to the Church of the Resurrection, on the top of Mount Calvary, where she was allowed to see a piece of wood said to be part of the true cross. There were a great number of pilgrims in the little town, and quite a crowd of these were kneeling round the sacred wood; but Imogene, in her simplicity, lifted her heart and eyes from the cross to Him who had hung upon it, for the lessons of simple faith she had learned from the lips of Placidia had remained uncorrupted through all these years, and Imogene regarded the cross only as a sacred symbol, not an object to be worshiped, as so many seemed to consider it now.

To be traveling once more along the great Roman road, that had been cut over hills and through intervening valleys straight on to the capital of Syria, Damascus, was her greatest anxiety, for

228

here she might overtake Placidia and her friend, she had heard, as they intended to rest there before proceeding to Antioch.

It was, therefore, with little regret that she bade her kind hosts farewell, and, taking the little wallet of food they had provided for her journey, started once more across the hills of Judea toward the level plain beyond. Imogene was again weary and footsore before the last hill was climbed, for the great highways never turned a hair-breadth to avoid an eminence, but went straight on, over and through every obstacle, nothing being allowed to turn them aside.

When, at length, the last hill was gained, and Imogene saw a level plain stretching on for miles before her, she took heart again, for this would not be such weary walking, although she would lose the pleasant glimpses of budding trees in the orchards and the musical splash of little brooks as they came tumbling down the sides of the hills, for the plain was barren and sterile, and there were no wandering shepherds leading their flocks to pasture on the few blades of stunted grass that grew here. So, if her feet grew less weary, her eyes pined for the pleasant variety of hills and valleys, rocky ridges and green cornfields.

At length, after three days of weary tramping, the white towers of the longed-for city rose gradually above the horizon; but before the city gates were reached her weary eyes were refreshed by the sight of rich gardens and forests of

WALLET: *knapsack*
EMINENCE: *hill*

olive-trees, palms, and Damascus plum-trees, for here the plain was watered by the "golden stream," the Abana and Pharpar, fresh from their home amid the snows of Lebanon. Well might the Eastern writers call this Syrian capital, "a pearl surrounded by emeralds," for with its forest fringe of walnut, fig, pomegranate, plum, apricot, citron, pear, and apple trees growing in richest luxuriance, and its never-failing streams of purest water, Damascus, though on the borders of a desert, is one of the loveliest spots on earth.

Even Imogene forgot her weariness and disappointment for a time, lost in admiration at the scene, for the trees were now of the freshest green, many of them bursting into blossom, so that even the roadside hedges and forest looked like one vast garden, while in the midst rose the marble domes and towers of the ancient city.

Imogene had little difficulty in passing the guard at the gates, for her kind and thoughtful friends at Jerusalem had given her a letter to be delivered to the Christian brethren at the hospital of Damascus, recommending her as a sister in need, who was traveling to Antioch without means, having been robbed on her journey of all the money she possessed.

This letter secured her entrance at the great eastern gate, and she was soon pushing her way through the long, straight, busy street, that traverses the whole length of the city. It was in this same street that Paul lodged when he came hither

on his persecuting errand from the Sanhedrin of
Jerusalem, and it was within sound of a similar
din from mule-drivers and camel-leaders, and all
the jostling, bustling noise of a commercial city,
that his first prayer arose to heaven. In this street
the hospital for sick and destitute travelers had
likewise been established, and Imogene hastened
her steps toward it with all speed, for the sight of a
fair-haired British slave was not so common here,
and her appearance was arousing a degree of attention anything but pleasant. So she presented
her letter as soon as she could, and was at once admitted to the rest and refreshment of this home,
which Christian benevolence had provided for the
poor and destitute.

The deacons of the Church here were at once
informed of the object of Imogene's journey, and
while she was resting and recruiting her strength,
they and their brethren, the parabolani, were making inquiries throughout the city for the travelers
who had preceded her.

After three days, during which Imogene had
been carefully nursed and her clothes washed,
so that she might recommence her journey thoroughly refreshed, the news was brought to her
that the widow, Arethusa, with her friend, Placidia, had tarried a week at Damascus, but had gone
on to Antioch, and must have reached that city
long since. Imogene was told now of the regulation that had been adopted of not allowing any

SANHEDRIN: *council of Jewish judges*
RECRUITING: *recovering*

beggars or indigent strangers to pass the gates of Antioch, and for a moment her heart died within her, for she knew that by the time the rest of her journey was accomplished she should be in the forlorn condition of a ragged, penniless beggar, although the trusted household slave of a wealthy merchant, who had provided her with an ample supply of money for all her needs.

She could not wholly restrain her tears as she thought of the possibility of disappointment when her errand was so nearly accomplished, but her faith did not fail her entirely. "I will press on to Antioch," she said, speaking to the deacon who had told her of the cruel regulation, "and if thou wilt give me a letter to Placidia, telling her the messenger from Alypus of Tagaste awaits her outside the city gates, I shall have little fear but the Lord will provide the rest."

"Thou shalt have the letter, with a good supply of dried dates and a bottle of wine, for thy journey," said the deacon; and giving her as his parting words the first verse of the Twenty-third Psalm, to ponder over by the way, he went to prepare the letter and order the provisions, while Imogene murmured the sacred words softly to herself lest she should forget them: "The Lord is my shepherd; I shall not want."[1]

"No, I shall not want," she repeated, "even as a beggar outside the gates of Antioch; He will provide for me."

---

[1] PSALM 23:1

INDIGENT: *poor*

Chapter XX

The Meeting of Friends

JOHN CHRYSOSTOM, with another young reader of the Church of Antioch, was returning from a visit to the cemetery near the ruined shrine of Daphne, when near the city gates they were hindered by the gathering of a little crowd round a poor woman who seemed to be in great distress, and was crying bitterly.

"It is a cruel law," exclaimed one of the bystanders just as the two boys stopped, "but it is useless to appeal to the guard; thou mightest as well plead with the head of Charon yonder, as think of touching a soldier's heart."

"What is it?" asked John of one of those standing near.

"Nothing new, as thou mayest see," replied his companion, who had edged himself forward to get a nearer view. "It is only a beggar woman trying to get into the city;" and he would have hurried forward at once, but John still lingered.

"Nay, nay; the poor woman would be content if

her letter was taken within the city," said the man
to whom John had first spoken, "but the guard re-
fuses to take charge of it."

"Will she entrust it to me, think you? I am going into the city, and will carry it to whomsoever it
concerneth," said John.

"She will doubtless be glad to have it taken by
any means. Move aside, good friends, and let this
young citizen speak to the woman," and as he
spoke the man pushed the lad forward through
the little crowd of idle, curious gazers.

John understood the reason of their curiosity
when he stood face to face with the stranger, for
her blue eyes and fair hair were an unwonted sight
in the neighborhood of Antioch; and for a moment he, like the rest, could only stand and gaze
at her in speechless surprise.

She did not seem to notice the curiosity her appearance had excited; but when John drew near,
she said anxiously,

"Art thou a citizen of Antioch?"

"Yes, I dwell there with my mother," said John,
answering her in Greek, which she spoke with a
slightly foreign accent.

"Wilt thou deliver a letter for me to a noble lady
of the city, named Placidia? and she will, doubtless, reward thee for thy trouble, for she hath long
expected my arrival."

"Placidia!" repeated John, taking the letter from
her hand as he spoke, and looking at the woman

UNWONTED: *unusual*

still more curiously. "From whom dost thou bring this letter?" he asked.

"From the Church of Damascus," answered Imogene, trembling with anxiety lest he should refuse to take it. "If thou wilt deliver it to one of the deacons of the Church he will place it in Placidia's hands."

John smiled. "I can carry it to Placidia," he said; "she dwelleth with my mother in the city."

"Thou dost know my Placidia!" exclaimed Imogene, in a transport of delight; "thou hast seen her, and knowest she is well!"

"Yes, she is well," said the lad in a tone of astonishment, wondering not a little how this stranger could know Placidia.

"Thou wilt take the letter to her, then, and tell her Imogene, the Briton, hath journeyed hither from Tagaste."

"Thou comest from Alypus of Tagaste," said John quickly.

Imogene bowed her head. "Alypus is my master, and I have journeyed hither in his stead," she said; "hasten with the letter to Placidia, and I will tarry here until she comes."

"Nay, nay; but thou shalt come with me," said John, and he escorted Imogene once more to the city gates. But at the outer wall they were met with a blank refusal from the guard, who looked angrily at Imogene for daring to present herself before him again.

IN A TRANSPORT OF DELIGHT: *carried away by delight*

"Nay, nay; speak not so roughly," said John. "She is no beggar, but a true woman and a trusty slave, who hath been robbed on her journey hither."

"And what art thou, bold boy?" asked the guard, with a half-amused, half-angry smile.

"I am plain John Chrysostom, the son of Arethusa, and a reader of the Church in Antioch," replied the lad fearlessly.

"Thou art John of the smooth tongue and bold speech," retorted the man; "but I cannot let the woman pass."

John turned away, looking greatly disappointed amid the laughter of the bystanders, who repeated the nickname: "John of the smooth tongue."

The city was famous for its bestowal of nicknames, and it was through this propensity of the Antiochians that the followers of Jesus were first called "Christians." Another bestowed by them a few years later on this young reader of the Church has come down to our own time, and Chrysostom is everywhere known as the "Golden-mouthed Preacher," or "John of the Golden Mouth."

Of his future eminence and popularity, however, the citizens knew nothing at present, and so it was amid a shower of laughs and jeers from those who were hurrying through the gates that he turned back with Imogene, assuring her that Placidia would come to her with all possible speed.

He hastened home with the letter as quickly as possible, causing quite a commotion in the quiet

PROPENSITY: *natural inclination*
EMINENCE: *fame*

household by his account of the crowd gathered round Imogene, and the refusal of the guard to allow her to pass the city gates.

"A messenger from my Alypus at last," said Melissa, rousing herself from her habitual, indolent indifference as John spoke of this.

"Thou must fetch her home, my Placidia; she needs rest and refreshment after her weary journey," said the gentle widow, while Placidia was reading the letter and repeating the name, "Imogene," in a sort of unconscious wonder that highly exasperated John, who, in his impatience, would have dragged her out of the house at once.

"Nay, nay, my son; be not so impatient; if this poor woman is so weary she will not be able to walk through the city, and Placidia had better fetch her home in the litter."

This suggestion was acted upon, and the palanquin at once ordered to be brought out; while Placidia, in a maze of wondering surprise, prepared herself for the meeting with her old companion, for she doubted not but that it was the Imogene sold by old Deborah to the Empress Helena.

She alighted from her litter at the city gates, and walked forward alone to meet her old friend, wondering whether Imogene would recognize her in spite of the changes age had made in her appearance. There was little fear of her mistaking the British slave, for the fair hair and blue eyes were not likely to alter very much, and John had spoken of them the moment he reached home. She was not prepared for the full and joyful recognition she received; for, before she had reached the secluded spot to which John had directed her, Imogene came forward, and with a joyous cry of "Placidia, my Placidia!" threw herself upon her bosom and burst into tears.

"Imogene, I never thought to meet thee on this side of the river of death," said Placidia as soon as she could speak, and then they embraced again, until at last Placidia half-led, half-carried poor Imogene to where she had left the slaves with her litter, for the poor woman was so weary from her long journey that the excitement of this meeting was almost too much for her feeble strength.

As soon as they reached home her wants were tenderly and carefully supplied, and not until she had somewhat recovered would they allow her to talk even of Alypus or her journey.

At length, however, Melissa was allowed to ask her as many questions as she liked about her son and grandson and their residence in Tagaste, and the following day Placidia and Imogene spent some hours together, talking over the events of the past thirty years, for each was anxious to know what had befallen the other.

"Thou didst not go to the far-off Britain, as the empress-mother intended," said Placidia.

"Yes, I went with the Roman legion that were about to depart for Verulam soon after we were

VERULAM: *a city in southern Britain*

parted at Jerusalem, but the centurion and his wife who had taken charge of me did not set me at liberty, as Helena commanded. She was not a hard mistress, however, and my life at the Roman colony was pleasant enough, for Verulam had changed since the first martyr of Britain, the citizen, Albanus, was put to death for confessing himself a Christian. It is said that the name of the city is to be changed from Verulam to St. Alban's, in honor of the martyr. Hundreds in the town attend the Church that was erected upon the spot where he was slain, and lived and loved as brethren."

"Even as we did in Alexandria until Arius began teaching his pestilent heresy," said Placidia with a sigh.

"Nay, but I heard as I journeyed hither that one had begun to teach error even in our far-off Britain. Pelagius, a minister of the Cymri, is teaching that men were not originally sinful and can attain perfection, and this hath caused much unhappiness and division, so that men who are learned, instead of teaching the ignorant—those who still hold in reverence the forest spirits or the old gods of Rome, as so many do—spend their time in disputing with each other."

Placidia sighed. "One would think that disputation and not love was the fulfilling of the law."

"The love of many hath waxed cold,"[1] said Imogene, "and the world would doubtless be the better for less doubtful doctrine and more Christian

[1] MATTHEW 24:12
PESTILENT: *harmful*
CYMRI: *people of Wales*

practice; but the woe cometh through those who teach the perilous doctrine, and it behooveth all who love the Lord Christ in sincerity to withstand evil teachers as well as evil doers."

"Thou speakest truly, Imogene; but it seemeth to me that little hath been accomplished even by councils in any matter of dispute. I have heard of several at which little was accomplished beyond the mere talking of bishops and deacons."

"But how is the Church Catholic to be ruled and guided except by the voice of all her bishops assembled in council! For one man—bishop, patriarch, or pope—to do this would be far worse than being ruled by councils. I have heard that the Bishop of Rome and the Patriarch of Constantinople are even now trying to gain that power each for himself, each seeking to be a lord over God's heritage, instead of a shepherd feeding his flock."

Placidia smiled. "Rome and Constantinople are not all the world, they are only cities of one great empire, my Imogene; and though their bishops may think they are chiefs in the Church because they dwell in the mightiest cities, the rest can afford to smile at the mistake, for they know it is a mistake, and an assumption of power they do not possess."

"But if the empire should be divided again, as it was between the sons of Constantine, these rival cities and rival bishops may claim the preeminence, and what has been yielded by courtesy as a

mere harmless assumption may be claimed as an
absolute right, and the power thus gained may be
used by and by."

But Placidia shook her head. "These are not your
own thoughts, Imogene," she said with a smile.

"They were my husband's, and I often heard him
say that the pride of the bishops and their love of
power would bring trouble upon the Church."

"Then thou hast a husband in Tagaste?"

"Nay, my husband lies near the church of Verulam, in Britain. I have been a widow for many
years."

"And thy husband, was he a slave?" asked Placidia.

"Yes, but our marriage was blessed by the bishop," said Imogene, with a touch of pride; "we were
the first slaves in Britain to whom this honor was
granted."

"It was a rare occurrence at first, I know; it hath
grown more common of late. But tell me something of thy married life."

For a few moments the blue eyes were dimmed
with tears, and Imogene could only shake her
head sorrowfully. "My Publius and our babe both
died in less than two years after our marriage,
and for a time I rebelled and repined against the
will of God; but I learned afterward that it was in
mercy they were taken home to the Master's house
above, for Publius belonged to another family, and
when the legion to which my master belonged was

ordered to return to Rome I was taken with them, and so God, having taken my treasures into His own keeping, I was saved the more bitter pain of leaving them in Verulam."

"And so thou wast taken to Rome once more," said Placidia, tenderly smoothing the bands of fair hair that had lost the bright luster she had thought so beautiful.

"Yes, I stood up again in that horrible slave market and was bought by a merchant and taken to Tagaste. That was nearly ten years since, but they have been peaceful, profitable years, for Alypus is not a hard master, and to teach his son, my Adeodatus, the truths I learned from thy lips hath been a pleasant task."

"And does the Church of Tagaste still flourish?" asked Placidia.

"Yes. I would that thou couldst come to Tagaste, thou wouldst love Monica, the wife of Patricius Augustinus, one of the officers of the town," said Imogene warmly.

"Thou dost love her I can see, my Imogene," replied Placidia.

"Yes, if all Christian women were like Monica the world would be the better and the happier, for they would teach by their example, even as she doth, and the hardest hearts would be turned from evil, even as her husband's hath of late."

"Her husband is not a Christian, then."

"Nay, he is a worshiper of the old Egyptian

gods, Iris and Horus. Their son is the friend of my Adeodatus, and though I sometimes fear he will teach him much evil, I cannot tell Monica I deem the young Augustine a bad companion, for I know her heart is set upon seeing him converted to God, and that she is glad to see her son with Adeodatus as much as possible."

"Then this young Augustine will be much with thy charge while thou art absent," said Placidia.

"Too much, I greatly fear, and so thou wilt not deem me anxious to leave thee, my Placidia, if I hasten from Antioch as soon as I can."

"Nay, I would not detain thee an hour from thy duty, but thou must stay and rest a few days, and we will send thee by ship back to Egypt. It may be I shall see thy friend Monica, for my sister is too feeble to journey so far now, and if she deem it wise to go to Alypus in the summer I will bring her on her way."

A few days afterward Arethusa and Placidia accompanied Imogene to Seleucia, the port of Antioch, about twenty miles distant, and here she embarked once more for a perilous voyage across the Mediterranean.

Chapter XXI

Athanasius

BEFORE Imogene reached Tagaste messengers had been dispatched from Antioch to all the cities of the Roman empire bearing the intelligence that the expedition against the Persians had proved a most disastrous one, and that Julian had been killed in making a retreat into Armenia. There was scarcely a decent appearance of mourning anywhere for the emperor throughout his vast domain, for although he was gifted, learned, and the most active of the Cæsars, he was the least successful in carrying out his plans, and so his rule had been a series of attempts and ignominious failures that earned him the contempt of his subjects, while his oppressive edicts against the Christians, and his openly avowed determination to crush out their faith, caused his death to be rejoiced over by not a few. Alexandria celebrated the event by fetching back her banished patriarch, Athanasius, and once more installing him in the episcopal chair with every mark of public honor and rejoicing.

EPISCOPAL: *bishop's*

The priests of Serapis in vain threatened the city with the vengeance of the gods of Egypt, reminding them that Christianity was no longer the national religion. The crowds that flocked to the churches once more proved that it was the religion of the people now, whatever the State might profess and uphold; and the Serapium, where ignorant priests went through their mummeries of sacrifice, and the museum, with its garden of plane trees, where philosophers had walked and taught since the days of Euclid and Ptolemy Philadelphus, were alike deserted, so eager was everyone to hear who the successor of Julian was likely to be, for he had left no children to succeed him, and whether Paganism or Christianity was to be the national faith depended upon the will of their future emperor.

Alypus had just returned to his native city when this news came from Antioch, and he, with Quadratus, were among the most forward in welcoming the return of Athanasius. But for this Quadratus would have been on his way to Jerusalem, for he had grown weary of awaiting inactive the return of Imogene, and had decided to go himself and search for his sisters; but he agreed to defer his departure a short time longer now, as affairs were so unsettled in the city, and the death of Julian so far modified his own plans that he decided to journey direct to Antioch in search of Melissa and Placidia, feeling sure that they would return thither as

MUMMERIES: *empty ceremonies*
PTOLEMY PHILADELPHUS: *King of Egypt in the third century* B.C.

soon as the tidings of Julian's death reached them.

The suspense as to who the future emperor would be was not of long duration, for another messenger arrived from the frontier shortly afterward bringing the news that Jovian, one of the imperial guards, had been proclaimed by the army, and their choice had been confirmed by all the principal cities.

Jovian was almost unknown except to Quadratus, and he was surprised that his former companion in arms had been chosen to wear the purple, for there was nothing very remarkable about him except his cool courage in fighting and his dispassionate moderation in debate. It was this, it seemed, that had saved the Roman arms from utter defeat, and he had succeeded in making better terms with the Persian monarch than was at first expected, which was all the soldiers who had proclaimed him emperor cared for.

Not so the peaceable citizens of the towns and villages, who were being impoverished by the heavy taxes levied by Julian to pay for the daily sacrifices in the pagan temples—herds of fat oxen and hundreds of the choicest and most expensive birds being slaughtered daily in honor of Iris and Serapis, Apollo and Venus, while the poor were left to starve, and the struggling traders almost ruined by the heavy imposts.

To them the most important question was, whether Jovian would carry on the policy of Ju-

DISPASSIONATE: *calm*
IMPOSTS: *import taxes*

lian or return to that of the Christian emperors. To Athanasius, now getting on in years and worn down by trouble and persecution, it was as important as to the poorest fruit-seller who had only just paid for his own liberty out of the profits made by selling watermelons and pistachios, and so it was a great relief when his old friend Quadratus told him that Jovian had been a true and earnest Christian, with a strong dislike of the Arians, when they had served together in the wars of Constantine.

This last intelligence was most gratifying to Athanasius, and he determined to journey to Antioch with all speed to meet and welcome the new emperor. Such an opportunity as this was not likely to be missed by Quadratus, who was so anxious about his sisters' welfare, and so he prepared at once to leave Alexandria in the train of the patriarch, promising to return with Athanasius if possible, and bring Melissa and Placidia with him.

Alypus greatly desired to go, too, but his wife and business together rendered it impossible, and so he had to content himself by sending a costly present to his mother and gifts to the friends with whom she had been staying.

Meanwhile Antioch had begun to assume something of her former appearance. The death of Julian had been the signal for opening the prison doors to many Christians in Antioch, and as soon as the news came of Jovian's election, and that he was a Christian, the churches were again opened and public thanksgiving services were held.

None rejoiced more sincerely over the altered state of things than Arethusa and Placidia, although they had suffered but little themselves compared with many others during the late persecution, and none prepared with greater zest for the public rejoicings to be held in honor of the new emperor than the widow and John Chrysostom.

Each time he returned home now it was with some fresh item of news concerning the movement of the troops toward Antioch, or of some new device being prepared for the adornment of the city at the coming festival, for Antioch was not a little proud of the honor of being the first city to welcome Jovian.

Placidia often listened incredulously to these items of gossip, or shook her head with a grave smile that was very provoking, John thought, and he declared that she cared for nothing and no one but prisoners, beggars, and lepers.

"But these poor people have few to care for them," said Placidia, laughing outright at John's vexation; "and then I cannot feel much interest in news that I do not believe."

"Do not believe!" repeated John.

"Nay, I cannot believe thy last tidings—that the Patriarch of Alexandria is coming hither to welcome our new emperor," said Placidia with a slightly heightened color.

"And wherefore not, my Placidia?" said John, who noticed the signs of agitation in her face. "Is it that the great Athanasius would grudge the trouble of journeying so far?"

"Nay, the trouble would be little thought of if good could be done. But why should Athanasius journey so far?"

"To join in the frolics of our citizens at the festival," said John, with a roguish smile, and he was himself so amused at the idea of the grave, learned bishop disporting himself under the marble colonnades of their streets that he burst into a merry laugh, in which Placidia and his mother both joined.

"Athanasius would not need to come to Antioch to witness games and shows," she said; "our Alexandria will, without doubt, indulge in a splendid festival—"

"Or a riot," interrupted John mischievously, for the great Egyptian city was gaining for itself a rather unenviable notoriety in this particular. "But, Placidia," continued the lad more seriously, "dost thou not think Athanasius would be very anxious to know whether our new emperor is an Arian or one of the true Catholic Church?"

"Doubtless he is extremely anxious about this," admitted Placidia, "but still I cannot think—"

"Thou needest not to think, for it is sure and certain that our bishop with his clergy are going forth, by the road to Seleucia, to meet the great Egyptian patriarch," said John triumphantly.

"Art thou sure of this, my son?" asked Arethusa.

"So sure, my mother, that I am to walk with the

readers of the Church in the procession."

To Placidia, who had not seen Athanasius for more than thirty years—not since the time when he, as a simple deacon of the Church of Alexandria, came to visit her aged mother, the news seemed too good to be true, and yet when she reflected upon the visit lately paid to them by Imogene nothing seemed impossible. "My friends seem to have died and been buried for thirty years and then suddenly to have come to life," she said with something of a smile.

"Then, that is why my word is doubted!" said John with mock indignation. "Because Athanasius is thy friend he is not to be allowed to come to Antioch."

"Nay, I said not so," answered Placidia, "but it is passing strange that after thirty years of death-like silence one after the other of my old friends should reappear. Melissa came first; then Victor, the prisoner, who was liberated on sacrificing to Apollo; then Onias, the Jew, whom I saw so often with old Deborah; then Imogene, whom I always thought of as in the far-off Britain; and now our patriarch, Athanasius. It is marvelous."

"I wish Quadratus would reappear," said Melissa fretfully. "I must journey to Tagaste and see my Alypus this summer, and who is to go with me?"

"I will, my sister," said Placidia. "I say not that I will stay with thee," she added as she glanced fondly at Arethusa, with whom this matter had been previously talked over, "but I will certainly journey with thee to Tagaste and see thy Alypus."

Both sisters had questioned Imogene as to whether any tidings had reached Tagaste concerning their brother, but she had not heard the name of Quadratus.

As John had said, a procession issued from the gates of Antioch to meet the patriarch of Alexandria, scarcely less splendid in its appointments than the municipal one that went forth to meet the emperor, for, however plainly the bishops might live in the privacy of their own homes, they made a public display of wealth, quite unknown in the present day.

The bishops and archdeacons rode on white mules, richly caparisoned in embroidered silk, all the harness chains being of gold, while their own dress blazed with jewels. Behind came the deacons and presbyters in their various robes, and then the readers and choristers of the different churches in the city, for Athanasius was looked upon as the true and loyal champion of the Church in all her struggles against the encroachments of the temporal power, and must be met with all honor.

Placidia went with Arethusa to a friend's house, from the windows of which they could see the procession on its return with the great Egyptian patriarch, but Melissa declared she was unequal to the exertion, and so Quadratus passed the window where his sister stood quite unrecognized, for Placidia's whole thought was given to the gray-haired, somewhat diminutive, man, whose life had

MUNICIPAL: *government*
CAPARISONED: *decorated*

seen such strange vicissitudes, but whom all Antioch delighted to honor today.

Athanasius saw little of the gaping crowd that lined the streets and shouted a welcome to him as he rode past on a mule with similar trappings to that of their own bishop, for his mind was full of what he had heard concerning the bitter persecution of the previous winter, and the wonderful meekness and patience of the Church of Antioch in abstaining from revolt or riot, or resorting to any unlawful means of redressing their wrongs; for they were not the feeble power in the State they once were, which made their submission to the unjust edicts of Julian all the more remarkable.

Quadratus, on the other hand, was eagerly looking right and left in the hope of seeing one or both of his sisters, but it was difficult to recognize anyone in the motley throng, and so he passed on in the ecclesiastical train while Placidia watched him from a window close by, for his bronzed, weather-beaten face had attracted her attention, as well as his unclerical dress, but she had no idea that it was her brother.

After the meeting of the bishops came the welcoming of the new emperor, and Quadratus found himself once more in the midst of old friends and companions-in-arms.

Many of these seemed shy of meeting him at first, for they had only retained their position in the army by burning incense to the gods—a concession Quadratus indignantly refused to make, and

DIMINUTIVE: *small*
REDRESSING: *making right*

retired from his post rather than do violence to his conscience. Many, however, thought it a slight matter to sprinkle a little fragrant powder on the sacred flame as they passed before Julian, and as this was all that was required of them they yielded, and so in a few hours the army became pagan and devoted to the service of the gods of the empire, according to the emperor's belief. This same army had left Antioch as pagan but it returned from Persia Christian almost to a man, and one of the first acts of the new emperor was to restore the sacred ensign of the cross to its place of honor, and that Quadratus should be once more chosen as a guard of the labarum was not at all surprising to those who knew him.

Athanasius rejoiced at the honor thus conferred upon his old friend, but he was still more pleased to find the emperor so devoted to the Church, and so ready to uphold the famous Nicene Creed, which he looked upon as the great bulwark of religious truth, and to uphold which he had braved the anger of emperors, and risked both life and liberty.

Having secured the emperor's promise to uphold this against the Arians of the empire, Athanasius prepared to return to Alexandria, but Quadratus preferred to remain at Antioch a little longer, for he had not found his sisters yet, and he was determined not to return without them.

BULWARK: *protector*

Chapter XXII

Conclusion

THE Christian schools of Antioch were soon reopened, and the Scripture readings in the chamber of the church resumed. The church itself had been stripped of most of the gold and jewels that had adorned its walls and pillars, but the marble Christ still occupied its place above the altar; and the sacred emblems of the dove, the fish, the ship, and the cross within the circle, and the shepherd with his flock being painted in fresco along the sides, could not be removed when the church was ransacked of its treasures, and remained almost uninjured.

John Chrysostom was on his way to the reader's chamber once more, when, as he was passing through the church, he was surprised to see Athanasius standing near the altar at the upper end looking intently at the statue above. Seeing the lad, however, he came toward him, and John bowed in lowly reverence as he stood aside for him to pass. But instead of passing, Athanasius stood still before him.

"Thou art one of the readers," said the patriarch; "dost thou know John Chrysostom?"

Pride and pleasure brought a quick glow to John's face at his name being known by the good bishop, and he said, with another inclination of the head, "I am John Chrysostom; can I do aught to serve thy holiness?"

"Dost thou know one Placidia? She is an aged woman now, and hath dwelt some years in Antioch, I ween."

"Is she a native of Alexandria?" asked John quickly, thinking how delighted Placidia would be when she heard that Athanasius had inquired for her.

"Yes; she was stolen from Alexandria many years since," replied the patriarch.

"Then it is our Placidia," said John, scarcely able to repress his delight; "God sent her to Antioch to be my mother's nurse and teacher, and mine, too."

"May God abundantly bless her work, and bless thee, my son!" said Athanasius; and he laid his hands upon the lad's bowed head, and lifting his eyes to heaven prayed fervently that an abundant blessing might be poured out upon him.

"I wished to become a monk," John ventured to say when he again raised his head, "but my mother says I had better be a Christian-lawyer, for they are more needed in these evil days."

"Thou knowest who hath said, 'Children, obey thy parents,'[1] said Athanasius; "do this, my son,

---

[1] EPHESIANS 6:1

WEEN: *suppose or imagine*

and teach by example as well as by thy readings, and thou shalt become a blessing to the world and a pillar of the Church. Now wilt thou tell me where I shall find Placidia?"

"I—I will lead thee to her," said John.

"Nay, nay, my son; but what will these do who are waiting for thee to read to them the words of life? Thou shalt tell me which way I shall go, and where thy home is, and doubtless I can understand," said Athanasius, with a slight smile.

John directed him which road to take through the city to the banks of the Orontes; but all the time he was reading from the parchment roll to the little crowd gathered to hear the sacred Word his thoughts would wander toward his home, and he wondered whether the patriarch would go alone to pay this visit.

It was a relief to him today when his time for reading had expired, and he hurried through the streets at a pace which made people look after him in some surprise, for the sun was getting high in the heavens now, and the heat made any exertion unwelcome. But John hardly paused to choose the shadiest spots today, but rushed on, sometimes in the shadows of the colonnade, sometimes in the road, whichsoever happened to be least crowded, and at length rushed into the cool inner court at home, hot and breathless.

"Is Placidia at home? Hath his holiness from Alexandria been here yet?"

Arethusa looked at her son with a smile. "Placidia will laugh at thee again," she said, "for thy wonderful news."

"But it is true, my mother. Athanasius was in the church this morning and asked me for news concerning Placidia, and will certainly come to visit her."

"Did he not inquire for me?" asked Melissa, who was lying on a pile of cushions near the fountain.

"Nay, he asked only for Placidia," replied John. "He had heard my name, Mother, for he asked if I knew John Chrysostom," he added, turning toward Arethusa.

"And he is coming here, thou sayest. It may be my Alypus hath desired him to seek me out," said Melissa, with a sigh.

Placidia was out visiting the prisoners, and it was with some impatience John awaited her return to impart his wonderful news. It was scarcely told before a slave entered, saying a soldier was in the vestibule asking for Placidia.

"A soldier!" exclaimed John, in a tone of disappointment, as Placidia smilingly shook her head at him as she went out with the slave.

In a few minutes, however, she returned, looking greatly agitated, and going to Melissa's side she said, "The labarum is to be the imperial ensign once more, Melissa, and the guards are in Antioch."

"The guards of the labarum!" repeated Melissa,

excitedly raising herself on her cushions. "Then Quadratus is here."

"Yes, Quadratus is here," said another voice at her side, and the war-worn, weather-beaten face of her brother was bent over her, and for a few minutes no one could speak for the full tide of joy that rushed in upon their hearts at this happy reunion.

A little later Athanasius paid a visit to the long-separated brother and sisters, to the great delight of John, although the proposal he made was by no means so agreeable to either him or Arethusa. She urged its adoption, however, regardless of the sorrow it would cause her to part with Placidia, for Athanasius had proposed that the sisters should return to Alexandria in the train of Quadratus. This plan would obviate many of the difficulties they would have experienced in traveling alone; and, indeed, the only mode of doing this in safety was for a large number to form themselves into one company, so that in the event of an attack by robbers they might, with their slaves, form a sufficient force to withstand them.

So it was arranged that Placidia should leave Antioch for a few months; but she promised to return before winter, for the thought of leaving Arethusa, whom she loved so dearly, was very bitter, while to the widow herself it was like a second widowhood to be thus separated from her foster-mother and dearest friend.

OBVIATE: *eliminate*

Quadratus found it hard to believe that the sunny-hearted, elderly woman, whose active love and service was known all over Antioch, could have been the cold, stately Placidia, to whom he appealed in vain on behalf of their dear mother. Truly God's ways were wonderful, and his methods of educating and guiding the human soul beyond man's understanding; for while Melissa had been cradled in luxury and had scarcely a wish ungratified, Placidia's days had been passed in the lowly service of a slave, and yet she was now by far the happier of the two sisters, for Melissa had grown peevish and fretful in the midst of her self-indulgence, and was now a far less happy woman than her active, self-forgetful sister.

Meanwhile Imogene had reached Tagaste in safety, where she found Adeodatus awaiting her arrival in the household of Monica. She was welcomed as warmly here as if she were Arethusa herself; and the story of her journey and its dangers was listened to with as much interest as though she had been the greatest lady in Tagaste. Even Patricius exerted himself for her convenience, and bade her stay until she had thoroughly recovered from the fatigue of her journey before proceeding on her way to Alexandria.

But Imogene was anxious to see Alypus and tell him the result of her journey, and likewise to remove Adeodatus as soon as possible from the society of Augustine, for the two boys were more intimate than ever now, and Adeodatus had learned

PEEVISH: *easily irritated*
SELF-FORGETFUL: *unselfish*

several bad habits from his companion, and, what
was worse, did not seem to suffer from any up-
braidings of conscience as Augustine did. This at
present was the only answer his mother received to
her prayers—he could not be happy in his sin; but
whether he would ever learn to hate it and turn
from it as a grievous and horrible thing, Monica
did not know. But she prayed on in faith and hope,
and we know that her prayers were not in vain, and
that Augustine, like Chrysostom, became a "burning and a shining light"[1] in the midst of a crooked
and perverse generation. Widely different was the
character of their boyhood, but they were alike
in this, they each had the inestimable blessing of a
pious mother, and so to Monica and Arethusa and
their quiet, unrecognized, undemonstrative piety,
may be traced blessings the full measure of which
can never be known.

At the time of which we write, however, it
seemed far more likely that the young Augustine
would prove a curse to those with whom he formed
any close friendship, and so it was not wonderful
that Imogene, in her watchful care of Adeodatus,
should wish to take him away from Tagaste as soon
as possible. But she heard, to her dismay, that Augustine would accompany them to Alexandria, for
Patricius had promised that he and Monica would
both visit Alypus this summer, and, of course,
their only son would go with them.

So Imogene was obliged to take refuge in prayer,
as well as Monica, that God would shield her dar-

[1] JOHN 5:35

ling from the evil of the world, and her prayer was answered, but not as she expected. As soon as they had landed on the quay at Alexandria they were met by the news that the plague had broken out in the city.

Patricius would have taken his wife and son back at once if he could, but this was impossible, and so he went through the half-deserted streets fearing each moment that the pestilence would seize upon him. Alypus, however, laughed at his fears, assured him that it was only in the poor quarter of the city that sickness was rife, and took him up to the tower that he might see how well-situated the house was for the sea-breezes to bear away all malaria or infection that might lurk in the air of the city. But, as if to prove the utter fallacy of all these assurances, the household was aroused that night with the tidings that Adeodatus had been seized with the plague, and before morning his life was despaired of.

Parthenia, who had never been a very fond mother, and had somewhat neglected her only son, was inconsolable now, and was with difficulty kept from disturbing her child, who lay quiet and peaceful in Imogene's arms, but could not bear to be separated from her. "Tell me about the blood of Christ taking away all sin," he panted between the spasms of pain, and then he added, "I have been a naughty boy at Tagaste, Imogene, and there is not time to cleanse my soiled baptismal robes by penance now, but the blood of Christ

RIFE: *common*

will cleanse us from all sin. I know it now, Imogene; I feel it here," and he laid his hand upon his breast.

"Yes, His blood is sufficient," said Imogene through her tears.

"Yes, for all sins—all sins," said the boy, faintly, and then he asked with sudden earnestness, "Why do we have to perform penance when the blood of Christ is sufficient? It makes us think it is not enough."

But Imogene could only shake her head. She was not wise enough to understand the reason of everything, and she could not say much, for her heart was overcome with the thought of parting with her charge in the very moment of their reunion, for she knew now that in a few hours Adeodatus would be beyond the reach of either sin or suffering—a blessed change for him, but making the world again dark and lonely to her.

Monica did all she could to soothe the grief of Parthenia, and she hoped the sudden death of Adeodatus would be blest to her son, warning him that he, too, might be called, and after a few hours' sickness be laid in the grave, and for a few weeks Augustine did seem somewhat seriously impressed.

Their stay at Alexandria was prolonged much beyond what they at first intended, but Monica was not sorry, for Parthenia clung to her more than ever now, so that she could be of some service to her friend, and then she likewise had a great desire to see and hear Athanasius, about whom she had heard so much, but who was absent on his visit to Antioch when they arrived. But his return was expected almost daily, and when he did arrive there was a double pleasure in store for Monica, for she and Placidia could not fail to be warm friends, and often spent hours in each other's company or with Imogene, for since the death of Adeodatus his nurse had found herself almost without occupation. That Arethusa and John should often be the subject of conversation was only natural, and Augustine asked numerous questions about the young reader of Antioch who was destined to be as widely known as the future Bishop of Hippo.

Monica could sympathize with Placidia's desire to return to Antioch very soon, for she could understand her love for Arethusa as well as the widow's love to Placidia; for she, too, owed it to the teaching of a faithful slave in her father's household that she was now rejoicing in the hope of eternal life, but she thought it was unwise to continue in a state of bondage, as Placidia had, and she quite approved of Quadratus' plan for liberating his sister and providing for her so far that she should be above want, even if Arethusa was taken away.

He was well-able to do this for he was a wealthy man, and Melissa would be taken care of by Alypus in the future, for Parthenia seemed much less exacting toward everybody since the death of her son, and so they were likely to live much more happily together. Finding that Quadratus was determined that she should share at least some portion of his wealth, Placidia arranged with Alypus for the redemption of Imogene that she might return to her native land. But Imogene shook her head sadly when this proposal was made to her. "I have no one in Britain who would care to welcome the worn-out British slave. What is freedom to me now when all my life hath been spent in captivity?"

"Then thou shalt come with me to Antioch," said Placidia. "I care not for liberty for myself, for I have been free for years except as love held me in chains; but for my brother's sake I must have my own dwelling now at Antioch, and thou shalt rule over it, Imogene, for I shall scarcely live less with my Arethusa because I am no longer her slave."

Quadratus could not stay long at Alexandria, for he had to proceed to Constantinople to meet the emperor, but before he went all the necessary arrangements were made concerning Placidia, and she and Imogene were placed under the protection of a party of travelers journeying to Antioch. Melissa was sorry to part with her sister, but as she and Parthenia were likely to live more happily together she did not grieve very deeply, for there were several things in which she and Placidia could not see eye to eye, especially in the adoration of the Virgin Mary, represented by the old statues of Venus, which Placidia had plainly spoken of as another form of idolatry.

Monica returned to Tagaste about the same time, and thus, after the wonderful reunion of friends that had taken place after this long separation, all returned to their own individual paths of duty, in the quiet performance of which they had found that happiness God alone could give, and the result of which was to be so far-reaching in its influence that it has not yet ceased, and will continue as long as the names of Chrysostom and Augustine are known and revered in the Church of Christ.

*   *   *

May the lessons taught by the unobtrusive lives of these women be pondered by many in these days of bustle and loud profession, and may we all learn from these lessons of the past to live more closely to Christ, to drink in more of His spirit of simplicity and love, and there will   be little danger of following the teachings of man or of falling into errors of either doctrine or practice! This was the cause of much, nay, of all the evil that crept into the early Church, and Churches are but individuals in the aggregate, for worldliness and evil would not be possible in a Church the individual members of which were simple, pure, and honest, caring for little beyond the opportunity to "sow beside all waters"[1] the knowledge of the love of God in Christ Jesus our Lord.

THE END

---

[1] Isaiah 32:20

ABOUT THE AUTHOR

Emma Leslie (1837-1909), whose actual name was Emma Dixon, lived in Lewisham, Kent, in the south of England. She was a prolific Victorian children's author who wrote over 100 books. Emma Leslie's first book, *The Two Orphans*, was published in 1863 and her books remained in print for years after her death. She is buried at the St. Mary's Parish Church, in Pwllcrochan, Pembroke, South Wales.

Emma Leslie brought a strong Christian emphasis into her writing and many of her books were published by the Religious Tract Society. Her extensive historical fiction works covered many important periods in church history. Her writing also included a short booklet on the life of Queen Victoria published in the 50th year of the Queen's reign.

Emma Leslie Church History Series

GLAUCIA THE GREEK SLAVE
A Tale of Athens in the First Century
After the death of her father, Glaucia is sold to a wealthy Roman family to pay his debts. She tries hard to adjust to her new life but longs to find a God who can love even a slave. Meanwhile, her brother, Laon, struggles to find her and to earn enough money to buy her freedom. But what is the mystery that surrounds their mother's disappearance years earlier and will they ever be able to read the message in the parchments she left for them?

THE CAPTIVES
Or, Escape from the Druid Council
The Druid priests are as cold and cruel as the forest spirits they claim to represent, and Guntra, the chief of her tribe of Britons, must make a desperate deal with them to protect those she loves. Unaware of Guntra's struggles, Jugurtha, her son, longs to drive the hated Roman conquerors from the land. When he encounters the Christian centurion, Marcinius, Jugurtha mocks the idea of a God of love and kindness, but there comes a day when he is in need of love and kindness for himself and his beloved little sister. Will he allow Marcinius to help him? And will the gospel of Jesus Christ ever penetrate the brutal religion of the proud Britons?

OUT OF THE MOUTH OF THE LION
Or, The Church in the Catacombs
When Flaminius, a high Roman official, takes his wife, Flavia, to the Colosseum to see Christians thrown to the lions, he has no idea the effect it will have. Flavia cannot forget the faith of the martyrs, and finally, to protect her from complete disgrace or even danger, Flaminius requests a transfer to a more remote government post. As he and his family travel to the seven cities of Asia Minor mentioned in Revelation, he sees the various responses of the churches to persecution. His attitude toward the despised Christians begins to change, but does he dare forsake the gods of Rome and embrace the Lord Jesus Christ?

www.SalemRidgePress.com

EMMA LESLIE CHURCH HISTORY SERIES

FROM BONDAGE TO FREEDOM
A Tale of the Times of Mohammed
At a Syrian market two Christian women are sold as slaves. One of the slaves ends up in Rome where Bishop Gregory is teaching his new doctrine of "purgatory" and the need for Christians to finish paying for their own sins. The other slave travels with her new master, Mohammed, back to Arabia, where Mohammed eventually declares himself to be the prophet of God. In Rome and Arabia, the two women and countless others fall into the bondage of man-made religions—will they learn at last to find true freedom in the Lord Jesus Christ alone?

THE MARTYR'S VICTORY
A Story of Danish England
Knowing full well they may die in the attempt, a small band of monks sets out to convert the savage Danes who have laid waste to the surrounding countryside year after year. The monks' faith is sorely tested as they face opposition from the angry Priest of Odin as well as doubts, sickness and starvation, but their leader, Osric, is unwavering in his attempts to share the "White Christ" with those who reject Him. Then the monks discover a young Christian woman who has escaped being sacrificed to the Danish gods—can she help reach those who had enslaved her and tried to kill her?

GYTHA'S MESSAGE
A Tale of Saxon England
Having discovered God's love for her, Gytha, a young slave, longs to escape the violence and cruelty of the world and devote herself to learning more about this God of love. Instead she lives in a Saxon household that despises the name of Christ. Her simple faith and devoted service bring hope and purpose to those around her, especially during the dark days when England is defeated by William the Conqueror. Through all of her trials, can Gytha learn to trust that God often has greater work for us to do *in* the world than *out* of it?

www.SalemRidgePress.com

Additional Titles Available From

Salem Ridge Press

YUSSUF THE GUIDE
Being the Strange Story of the Travels in Asia Minor of
Burne the Lawyer, Preston the Professor, and
Lawrence the Sick
by George Manville Fenn
Illustrated by John Schönberg

Young Lawrence, an invalid, convinces his guardians, Preston the Professor and Burne the Lawyer, to take him along on an archaeological expedition to Turkey. Before they set out, they engage Yussuf as their guide. Through the months that follow, the friends travel deeper and deeper into the remote regions of central Turkey on their trusty horses in search of ancient ruins. Yussuf proves his worth time and time again as they face dangers from a murderous ship captain, poisonous snakes, sheer precipices, bands of robbers and more. Memorable characters, humor and adventure abound in this exciting story!

MARIE'S HOME
Or, A Glimpse of the Past
by Caroline Austin
Illustrated by Gordon Browne R. I.

Eleven-year-old Marie Hamilton and her family travel to France at the invitation of Louis XVI, just before the start of the French Revolution. There they encounter the tremendous disparity between the proud French Nobility and the oppressed and starving French people. When an enraged mob storms the palace of Versailles, Marie and her family are rescued from grave danger by a strange twist of events, but Marie's story of courage, self-sacrifice and true nobility is not yet over! Honor, duty, compassion and forgiveness are all portrayed in this uplifting story.

www.SalemRidgePress.com

For Younger Readers

DOWN THE SNOW STAIRS
Or, From Goodnight to Goodmorning
by Alice Corkran
Illustrated by Gordon Browne R. I.

On Christmas Eve, eight-year-old Kitty cannot sleep, knowing that her beloved little brother is critically ill due to her own disobedience. Traveling in a dream to Naughty Children Land, she meets many strange people, including Daddy Coax and Lady Love. Kitty longs to return to the Path of Obedience but can she resist the many temptations she faces? Will she find her way home in time for Christmas? An imaginative and delightful read-aloud for the whole family!

SOLDIER FRITZ
A Story of the Reformation
by Emma Leslie
Illustrated by C. A. Ferrier

Young Fritz wants to follow in the footsteps of Martin Luther and be a soldier for the Lord, so he chooses a Bible from the peddler's pack as his birthday gift. When his father, the Count, goes off to war, however, Fritz and his mother and little sister are forced to flee into the forest to escape being thrown in prison for their new faith. Disguising themselves as commoners, they must trust the Lord as they wait and hope for the Count to rescue them. But how will he ever be able to find them?

AMERICAN TWINS OF THE REVOLUTION
Written and illustrated by Lucy Fitch Perkins

General Washington has no money to pay his discouraged troops and twins Sally and Roger are asked by their father, General Priestly, to help hide a shipment of gold which will be used to pay the American soldiers. Unfortunately, British spies have also learned about the gold and will stop at nothing to prevent it from reaching General Washington. Based on a true story, this is a thrilling episode from our nation's history!

www.SalemRidgePress.com

Historical Fiction by William W. Canfield

THE WHITE SENECA
Illustrated by G. A. Harker

Captured by the Senecas, fifteen-year-old Henry Cochrane grows to love the Indian ways and becomes Dundiswa—the White Seneca. When Henry is captured by an enemy tribe, however, he must make a desperate attempt to escape from them and rescue fellow captive, Constance Leonard. He will need all the skills he has learned from the Indians, as well as great courage and determination, if he is to succeed. But what will happen to the young woman if they do reach safety? And will he ever be able to return to his own people?

AT SENECA CASTLE
Illustrated by G. A. Harker

In this sequel to *The White Seneca*, Henry Cochrane, now eighteen, faces many perils as he serves as a scout for the Continental Army. General Washington is determined to do whatever it takes to stop the constant Indian attacks on the settlers and yet Henry is torn between his love for the Senecas and his loyalty to his own people. As the Army advances across New York State, Henry receives permission to travel ahead and warn his Indian friends of the coming destruction. But will he reach them in time? And what has happened to the beautiful Constance Leonard whom he had been forced to leave in captivity a year earlier?

THE SIGN ABOVE THE DOOR

Young Prince Martiesen is ruler of the land of Goshen in Egypt, where the Hebrews live. Eight plagues have already come upon Egypt and now Martiesen has been forced by Pharaoh to further increase the burden of the Hebrews. Martiesen, however, is in love with the beautiful Hebrew maiden, Elisheba, whom he is forbidden by Egyptian law to marry. As the nation despairs, the other nobles turn to Martiesen for leadership, but before he can decide what to do, Elisheba is kidnapped by the evil Peshala and terrifying darkness falls over the land. An exciting tale woven around the events of the Exodus from the Egyptian perspective!

www.SalemRidgePress.com

CPSIA information can be obtained at www.ICGtesting.com
Printed in the USA
LVOW070737240313

325713LV00001B/8/A

9 781934 671078